The Branded Heart

The Branded Heart

Michele E Fischer

TATE PUBLISHING
AND ENTERPRISES, LLC

Published by Tate Publishing & Enterprises, LLC
127 E. Trade Center Terrace | Mustang, Oklahoma 73064 USA
1.888.361.9473 | www.tatepublishing.com

Tate Publishing is committed to excellence in the publishing industry. The company reflects the philosophy established by the founders, based on Psalm 68:11,
"The Lord gave the word and great was the company of those who published it."

Book design copyright © 2015 by Tate Publishing, LLC. All rights reserved.
Cover design by Nino Carlo Suico
Interior design by Jomar Ouano

Published in the United States of America

ISBN: 978-1-62463-715-5
1. Fiction / Christian / General
2. Fiction / Christian / Western
15.08.11

To my family

Always remember
God Himself
is our greatest blessing!

In Memory of

My Mom and Feliz "the Fleece,"
two great bundles of joy in my life

Contents

1

Where Am I?

Monday, March 12, 1877

It's so cold at night! I almost can't stand it! The walls of their house are just board and batten wood and do not insulate. Though the air is freezing, heat hits my back from a blazing fireplace in my room. Fortunately, I used to sleep with my windows open in relatively cold weather; I've always been one for cold air and warm blankets.

But, here, when I wake up in the mornings, it's so cold I can hardly get myself out of bed. Then the days warm up, but somehow the house stays cool. Although, if the temperature is high outside and we have a fire going inside to cook, it can get unbearably hot in the house.

How conditioned I was to the temperature-controlled environment I came from! I feel like a wimp here. It doesn't seem to bother this family.

I found a slip of blank paper and a flat, square pencil in the nightstand by my bed (a straw-filled mattress on a frame latticed with ropes I have to tighten every night). This pencil is difficult to write with. I am writing (as best I can) my first diary entry. Perhaps one day I can get a real diary if I am here for a while. But where am I? Barlow, Arizona, I'm told. In the year 1877!

Okay. I'm either dreaming, dead, or gone crazy. All I remember is I went to bed in my apartment in Agoura Hills, California, in the good ol' twenty-first century only to be awoken the next morning by hard earth nicely warming my back and intense heat on my face. I was outside somewhere!

This was a sudden change from the chilled air I was breathing in my bed only a moment before. It was November where I came from, and I was snug under my heavy wool blanket Granny had crocheted me. It holds in body heat good. I wish I had it here for the nights!

I knew I was now outside, but I was afraid to open my eyes. I felt my Bible faced down on my stomach. That's right! I had been reading it when I fell asleep. Harsh sunlight finally pried my eyes open, blinding me, when a dark figure blocked out the sun. My vision sharpened, and the figure became clear; it was a man crouching over me.

He had a rugged, chiseled face with high cheekbones framed by an auburn mustache and beard. I'd never seen anyone who looked quite like him before. I was much taken by him and could scarcely look away. His eyes were shadowed by a dusty leather hat with a wide brim.

He muttered something then said it again. I heard him clearly the second time.

"Are you all right, miss?"

"I think so. Where am I?" I asked.

"On my ranch."

Warily I pulled myself up to look around. I was still in my night clothes: grey sweatpants and a turquoise thermal hoodie bought for day wear but destined to become a night shirt.

Sitting up, I saw dirt ground patched with dry grass as far as the eye could see. I spotted some cows or bulls in the distance. Definitely not Agoura Hills, California. This was a more arid and rocky terrain, not the rolling green-and-yellow hills freckled with oak trees I was used to.

Then I took a good look at this man. His clothes were old (antique old). And dirty enough. The material of his soft dark-blue shirt looked thin and just different. It was tucked in rough black pants (denim or canvas, I couldn't be sure). He wore brown leather suspenders and black dirt-caked boots. And his scent! He was close enough to smell it: a mixture of sweat and leather. I took him in with a deep breath and became fully here.

Timidly I reached out to touch his arm. He was real. This could not be a dream. I was completely awake. I know I was. He braced me as I got up on legs I began to feel. I was barefoot on the hot ground. Stones pricked my burning feet.

He observed me hopping about as he pulled up a saddled horse as black as night save a white diamond-shaped spot on its forehead. I thought I heard him call the horse Grant.

"Bes' get you on him, miss," he said.

He put his hands around the back of my waist and hoisted me up. I fiddled with the one stirrup, clumsily swinging my other leg over Grant's back. The man hopped on his saddle in front of me.

"Hold fast to me," he instructed.

I could have buried my face into the base of his neck and the length of his hair. Instead, I timidly put my arms around his small waist and clenched my arms as he jerked his horse into motion.

We rode across his dry land, my arms hugging him, breathing him in, completely silent.

Lord, if I am dreaming, I do not want to wake up.

Then a homestead came into view on the flat horizon. I saw a rancher-style house made of board and batten wood. It had a smoking stone chimney and a meager porch supported by crude beams clearly cut out of thin tree trunks.

A plain wood barn sat at the distant left with chickens bopping about it freely. Someone came out of the house in a long dark-blue skirt covered by a white waist apron (with eyelet at the bottom—pretty!) and a high-collared prairie blouse.

He's married! Figures.

The woman had golden hair tied in a bun and a look of concern on her pretty face. She was perhaps in her early thirties, maybe a few years younger than the man.

Then it dawned on me. I didn't know his name. Nor he mine. He halted his horse just short of the porch. I grew nervous. The woman was staring at me as the man helped me down.

As we approached her, I dropped my eyes to the ground.

"I found her near the herd," he told the woman.

"Are you all right, dear?" she asked me, her shock softening. But she still looked me over quizzically.

"Yes, ma'am," I near squeaked.

"Let us go in," the man said.

My feet were relieved to climb cooler wooden steps onto their dusty porch. We walked through the front door that smelled of cedar, I think.

It was darker inside than I anticipated. As my eyes adjusted from the bright sunlight outside, I made out a long wooden table framed by two benches and Windsor end chairs.

I heard the ticking of a clock and found it: a cuckoo hanging beside a rugged hutch filled with beautiful, blue-and-white-patterned China trimmed with red berries (lingonberries, I'm told).

A stone fireplace interrupts the house, smack in the center, with two black horsehair chairs and sofa adorning it. The house extends beyond the hearth to a kitchen area where I noticed a homemade counter with an iron pump and standing shelves holding canned goods and jars of pickled green beans and other vegetables. Dried red peppers, sage, other herbs and wild flowers, ironware, and kitchen utensils hung from the ceiling on iron hooks.

Three open doorways branched off behind the long table. Bedrooms, I presumed. It was all rather cozy.

We sat down at the long table: the man at the head, the woman and I opposite one another on benches.

"My name is Sam Egan. This is my wife, Sarah. And what be your name, miss?"

"Renee."

They looked at me. It's obviously not a common name around here.

"Twining," I added, as if that would make a difference.

"Well, Ms. Twining, how is it I came to find you lying insensibly in the middle of my ranch?" Mr. Egan asked rather sarcastically.

Sarah frowned at him.

And then my mind began to spin. What should I say? The truth? Where I was from? What I thought had happened? Should I ask if I were dreaming? Or dead?

"I don't know." I heard myself carefully reply.

Before I could think of something else to say, Sam blurted out, "Where do you live, Miss?"

"Agoura Hills, California."

Oops! Should I have said the state? By the look on their faces, probably not.

"California?" Mrs. Egan repeated.

"And how, Ms. Twining, have you traversed all the long way to Arizona, and to here, nigh a hundred miles from the nearest train depot?" Mr. Egan prodded.

"I don't know. I don't know how I got here," was all I could say, regrettably.

The couple looked at each other, at a loss.

"Well, miss, what be the last that you remember?" Sam asked.

Okay, that was easier.

"Sleeping. I was sleeping in my bed," I answered.

"In California," Mrs. Egan added.

"Yes," I affirmed.

"And then?" Sam prodded me.

"And then I was here," I feebly explained.

Sam squirmed in his seat, uncomfortably. "You don't recall anything else in between?"

"No."

They just stared at me until I thought to add for courtesy, "Sir."

"Your family must be searching for you," Sarah surmised.

"My family aren't around."

I left it at that.

"Oh, my humble apologies," she said.

"There is not a one who might be looking for you?" Sam rephrased.

I just sat speechless, afraid to expand on much more.

"No, no one." I frowned. "Sir."

Tuesday, March 13, 1877

They noticed I had a big appetite at supper tonight. I was starving and filled my plate with beef stew and ate it all with two biscuits. Mr. Egan commented on my big appetite, but

I got the feeling it wasn't with approval. I guess I will have to make myself eat less. I noticed their portions were pretty modest on their plates. Oh, boy.

Saturday, March 17, 1877

Sarah gave me an ink well, a fountain pen, and some paper— stiff paper. It's tricky getting ink into the tip of the steel pen, but I'm getting used to it. Sure makes my handwriting neater, yes? Gee.

I'm still in shock over being here. And I can't help but wonder if I'm dreaming. I mean, what else could it be?

It makes me giggle; they think I'm in my twenties! Now I've always been told I look a lot younger than my age but, let's just say, I'm probably ten years older than Sarah! Maybe I look a lot younger because I've never had kids? That's stupid! But I do wish I had children, maybe someday, Lord willing.

The Egans have two sons, Gunnar and Paul. Paul is a sweet kid of eight with a mop of dirty blond hair, big green eyes, and freckles. Gunnar stands a little taller than me with dark hair like his father. He is a lanky, handsome kid who is thirteen going on twelve! I don't trust him.

Oh, I can't stop looking at Sam. At supper tonight, I think I made him cross when he asked me again where I was from. This time, I added where I was originally from— Maryland—but then regretted it considering the cold look that came over his eyes.

"Did I say something wrong?" I uttered.

"Maryland is below the Mason–Dixon line," little Paul explained, as though proud to know it. "It's Confederate."

"Not anymore. The war's over, dummy," Gunnar chastised him for which Sarah softly scolded him.

"Did any of your relatives fight in the war?" Sam asked me.

"Well, all I know is my great…um, my grandmother," I stammered. (almost said "my great-great grandmother!), "Her family were Irish immigrants that had a mercantile in Virginia. And whenever the Union Army came down, they hid the children in the pickle barrels."

You could have heard a pin drop. Everyone just stared at me. I grew really nervous but continued my story as Granny had told me years ago.

"But I guess the kids were glad when the war was finally over 'cause they wouldn't have to smell like pickles anymore."

Ha. Ha. Ha. No one laughed. But Paul smirked until he saw how stern his pa was.

"Pa fought in the war. For the north," Gunnar stated stoically.

Now, I'm all for the north and glad they won because it ended slavery in America; and I've always hoped that my ancestors had northern sentiments then, too. But what else could I say? You made my great-great-grandmother smell like pickles?

At least my appetite had vanished so I could make peace by not eating any more dinner. Aye.

Sunday, March 18, 1877

My hair presents a challenge when I try to put it up in a bun.
I have so many layers in it. Sarah seemed uncomfortable the
first time she helped me put it up. She asked me what I had
done to my hair. Since I was at a loss for words, she took it
for trauma and posed the idea that perhaps some Indians had
attacked me and layered my hair. Well, if that's true, they did
a great job! I paid fifty bucks for this haircut!

But she didn't say "Indians," she said "savages." I hate
that term. The only way I can tolerate anyone being called a
savage would be, like, Fred Savage. I gracefully explained that
Indians were not savages at all; they are very wise people who
have tremendous respect for the Creator and all His creation.

It's true. Look at all the many ways they show gratitude
in all of their cultures, Native Americans. They always give
thanks to God.

Sarah asked me if I knew any Indians. Oh, yeah. I know
one who's an aerospace engineer at NASA. 'Course I didn't
tell her that.

"I must say," she said, "I marvel at the craftsmanship
of their weaving. I've seen their baskets the trader sells in
town. Never have I seen baskets made so tight and with such
intricacy. I'm told that some even hold water! Could that be
true? They are very beautiful."

"Yes, they are."

Tuesday, March 20, 1877

I'm getting a little better at getting up at the crack of dawn and building stamina with the vigorous chores they've asked if I would undertake, which I graciously accepted.

It's impressive to see Paul and Gunnar work so hard. These kids really have a strong work ethic. Without prompting, they get up with the sun and begin their chores, even before breakfast. All day long they work until sundown. Some days they do get some "down time" to go fishing or play around outside.

Evenings the family spend reading the Bible before going to bed. Sarah is trying to teach Paul to read. The boys always say "Yes, sir" or "Yes, Pa" to Sam and "Yes, ma'am" or "Yes, Ma" to Sarah. I've never heard them talk back or disrespect their parents in any way. They even ask to be excused from the table when they finish a meal. I remember doing that, too, as a kid. Man, I forgot all about that!

2

An Extra Hand for Sarah

Tuesday, April 10, 1877

Dear Diary,

I am writing my first entry in you
having brought you home from the
nearby town of Barlow yesterday.
At last! I was running out of paper.
We went to get foodstuffs, and I
found you in the tent of a trader
who sold, among other things, books.
And I paid only two pennies! The
Egans paid me this for all the help
I've been giving them on the ranch. So
I spent all my hard-earned cash
on you.

I've been here about a month now and have been wearing some of Sarah's old clothes: a white cotton blouse with a long faded-brown skirt, a light-pink-and-white-checkered apron, black cotton stockings and, yesterday, I got a pair of shoes! I've been walking barefoot up until now.

Now I will be able to do more afternoon chores outside with my feet protected from the hot ground.

Until now, aside from collecting eggs and milking the cow at dawn, I have been restricted to indoor chores. But I'm learning how to cook from scratch (and I mean scratch) and mend clothes!

With shoes now, I can go to the creek to draw two buckets of water (very heavy!) every morning and afternoon—a creek Sarah told me was only a "hop, skip, and a jump away." That hop, skip, and jump is a mile away!

This family is nearly self-sufficient with their livestock and garden. We have beef, chicken (sometimes fish when the boys go fishing), eggs, and milk. In the garden, they've grown green beans, potatoes, tomatoes, spinach, squash, onions, and blueberries.

Sarah wanted to grow lingonberries. Her parents are from Sweden so she grew up on them in Boston. But they don't grow well in the mostly hot and dry climates.

We only buy raw supplies when we go into town: sugar, salt, flour, or cloth. Sam talks about buying sheep someday so we'll have wool if ever they sell enough beef. Then I can spin yarn to crochet heavy wool blankets for the winter, which they are happy about. My Granny taught me how to crochet. It comes in real handy here!

I'm lightening Sarah's load, she tells me. Paul told me this is the happiest they've seen their ma in a long time. She can get more done in a day having help with all the egg-collecting, water-drawing, cooking, washing, cleaning, sweeping, sewing, feeding, and weeding. With an extra hand for Sarah, they can even grow twice as many vegetables as they could last year.

And then there's "him." Their father. Her husband. I can't take my eyes off him and I really try not to look at him, which is difficult when he's talking to me. There's just something about him, the way he looks, the way he is, that gets to me down to the pit of my stomach. I feel it every time I look at him. I don't know what it is that makes him affect me so deeply.

I am trying my best to avoid him as I do my chores. And I think I've found a system that works. In the morning, I time collecting eggs so that I slip in and out of the barn to get the basket just before he goes in with the boys to tack up the horses: Grant, Thunder, and Mazy. All the while, I'm hiding in the hen house, gathering eggs. Then as they bring the horses out of the barn, I slip back in to milk their cow, Clover.

Well, my strategy works perfectly unless Sam forgets something and returns. Then I am forced to bid him good morning, which I try to do without looking at him with my head practically under the cow's udder. I feel so guilty yet I can't wait until I see him again when he returns from the cattle for meals.

Oh, why am I here, Lord!

Saturday, May 5, 1877

I know it's been awhile but I had run out of ink and had to wait until we got to town again to get more from the stationery merchant's tent (from where I bought you, diary) owned by Henry O'Cuddy, an Irishman with a black mustache that twirls up at the ends. He hangs a wood sign outside that names his shop, Scribes & Readers.

The large tent is lined inside with crudely made shelves and big trunks stacked with books, diaries, all kinds of glass ink wells, ink pens, sand (to dry the ink with), lap desks, you name it. Oh, I wish I could buy a lap desk with neat compartments in it.

Okay, what I want to tell you about. Today! I went to their next door neighbors, the Townsends, who are five miles away. They have an odd concept of distance here. "Oh, they're right next door." Yeah, right.

Anyway, I called on them (as they say here) to swap some of our fresh green beans for soap Mrs. Townsend had made. Well, Mrs. T said that one of their sheep just today gave birth to a lamb and I'd find it in the barn. I'd never seen a baby lamb before so I couldn't wait. In the stall, I found the cutest little lamb, already standing, next to her mama. The perky, little thing was so adorable balancing on lanky limbs.

I was about to go when I happened to glance down and stopped. Right at the base of the stall door lay a scrawny lamb, with a tangle of limbs, stained from birth. I wasn't even sure if it was alive or not. I called for Mr. Townsend who was just outside.

"Oh, she can't feed that one. It can't stand. Maimed from birth," he explained.

"So what will happen to it?" I asked.

Mr. Townsend shrugged. It was just gonna die! I was so upset he said I could take it, if I wanted to. I had to! Without a thought to what the Egans might think, I picked up the poor thing (still breathing, thank goodness). It lay limp in my arms. Her whole body was unnaturally bent in a C shape, and the limbs looked crooked.

I wrapped her in my shawl. Mr. Townsend (feeling empathy, I guess) drew some milk from the mama sheep into a large jar for me to take as well. He said if she survived the first night or two on this milk, she might pull through.

The Egans were quite surprised to see me return with, not only a basket of soap, but a lamb. Paul was most intrigued. I convinced them that this sheep might one day provide the wool we need for me to make heavy blankets for the winter. Sarah agreed and further persuaded Sam that this may be the only way they may ever have a sheep since they are unable to afford to buy one.

I made a funnel out of cheese cloth and cut a tiny slit in a corner edge with a knife for the lamb to drink through: a cloth baby bottle.

She's so cute! I named her Feliz, thinking of Spanish names since she was born on Cinco de Mayo. She makes me very happy. I just cleaned her up. Now she's lying before the fire in my room, wrapped in my shawl, sound asleep.

Sunday, May 6, 1877

I slept with Feliz on my tummy under the covers all night to feed her the milk. Call it maternal instinct but I somehow woke up every few hours. When I fell asleep the last time, I did not know if by morning I'd have a dead lamb or a live one on my stomach.

But I prayed, and this morning she opened her eyes and lifted her head, as if to say, "Good morning!" Thank you, Jesus!

Wednesday, May 8, 1877

Feliz can stand now by herself but takes only a few steps and then plops down and that's it. It takes all her strength it seems. She's so feeble. I carry her everywhere I go and feed her the cow's milk now. Maybe Clover will adopt her. I'm just exhausted all the time having to feed her throughout the night and then get up early to start the day. Ugh. Motherhood is tough!

Friday, May 11, 1877

I sometimes have to use the bathroom in the middle of the night. As they don't have an extra chamber pot for me yet to keep under my bed (it's on the list for the next time we sell beef), I usually sneak out my window to go to the outhouse. I take my lantern because it is pitch-dark!

But up in the sky, you've never seen so many stars! Not thousands, not millions but billions. The entire sky is speckled with stars. It's like you're looking at the whole universe! And the cloudy Milky Way is so clear and massive! I've never seen it before in my entire life! I didn't even know it was possible to see from the earth without a telescope. It looks like a science-fictional sky on another planet! It took my breath away the first time I saw it. It always stops me in my tracks, no matter how bad I have "to go."

Saturday, May 12, 1877

Gunnar made a clever observation that I'm now wearing shoes and gleefully suggested that I would do well to muck out the stalls for him so he can be of greater service to Pa (I mean, Sam).

Unfortunately, his suggestion was unanimously accepted and I've taken upon the gruesome task. But I have to say, when the early mornings are freezing cold, which even in May they can be, steaming manure can be of great comfort with the heat it adds to the enclosure. Never in my life would I ever confess gladness for manure. But there you have it.

How's that for trying out their lingo?

Monday, May 14, 1877

Today I played with baby chicks that were just born. They like sitting in my apron. Oh, they're so cute! They look like little cotton balls hopping about. I sweet talk and mush over Feliz and all the animals here, even the steer. But I always get funny looks from the Egans (and the animals!). But I can't help it! They're "cutsy-pootses"! Paul always laughs when I say that.

Feliz is walking now! Her body and hind legs have straightened out, although the right hind hoof is bent like a foot. You could put a baby shoe on it. Her front right leg is bent inwards at the knee, but it sure doesn't stop her! When she has a lot of energy, she'll hop and stomp about on all fours like a deer or something. She loves chasing me or Paul around. She's so cute!

When I bathe her, her short wool is white as snow. She has golden irises around her cat-like pupils that just peer up at you in complete innocence. And those ears! Her ears hang like God put them on upside down; they look a little like the flaps on *The Flying Nun*'s cornette (headpiece on her habit) or Dobby's ears, the house elf in that Harry Potter movie.

I made diapers for her to wear inside at night, out of some old burlap they had in the barn (eck, I know). I cut a hole in it for her tail. Sam, especially, thinks I'm strange but it helps a little with her wetting the bed at night. Well?

Now she follows me around wherever I go as I do my chores. Perhaps I should change my name to Mary.

Tuesday, May 15, 1877

After supper, Sarah reads a few Bible verses and then sends the boys to bed. Then it's just Sam, she, and I sitting quietly around the blazing hearth. Feliz is either curled up on my lap or working her legs around the room.

Sarah knits and I am resigned to mending shirts or trousers, having yet to tackle knitting with two needles (I don't know how she does it). Sam cleans his rifle, sharpens knives, or tans leather. These people never stop working!

It's uncomfortable for me. I feel like my feelings are written all over my face. I'm so exhilarated by the sight of him but I try desperately not to appear so. It's shameful. But I'm usually the first of us three to go to bed, completely exhausted! Like now. Gotta feed Feliz and change her diaper. Good night!

Thursday, August 23, 1877

What excitement and mystery! We had a surprise visitor today on the Egan ranch—the pony express. (Though, I'm told the pony express has gone out of business but I don't know what else to call it). A young man with stuffed saddle bags on his horse rode up with a special delivery for Sarah. Gunnar exclaimed how rare this was because you usually have to inquire in town for your mail at the Barlow post office. It was unheard of for mail to be delivered at your door!

There was no return address on the envelope sealed with a glob of red wax that was impressed with the insignia of a pineapple between two laurels. Sam muttered that mark was common in Virginia. He insisted the delivery boy tell him from whom this letter came, but the boy did not know.

Without even opening it, Sam handed the letter right back, saying, "You have the wrong Sarah Egan."

I looked at Sarah, who was stunned but said nothing. She turned and went inside the house. Completely baffled, I followed her. She would say nothing more about it but pleasantly asked for my help with making bread for supper.

Saturday, May 19, 1877

Paul gave us a fright today. Eight years old and he leads the herd of steer out to grassier grounds. Well, he rides a brown horse with a white streak down her nose, Mazy, on a secondhand saddle that has broken billet straps. So, every day, Sam binds the bottom of the saddle with rope against Mazy's belly, over a piece of cloth to prevent rope burn.

Well, Mazy sweat so much today that the saddle slipped, and Paul slid right off of her into the running herd! By the grace of God, he was okay, just bruised up. Sarah rebuked Sam for letting Paul still use that saddle, but they just cannot afford a new one.

Thursday, May 24, 1877

My baby's in the barn! Sam made me put Feliz out there with Clover. Says she can't sleep in the house anymore. I hate him!

Friday, June 1, 1877

I am getting better at doing the ranch work. I am not collapsing in exhaustion so much when I go to bed now. You know? It's refreshing to wake up early (really early) knowing that I'm going to collect eggs from the hen hut, milk the cow, go to the creek for water, and muck stalls—well, except that, rather than sit in intolerable traffic and then in that stagnant-aired law office, I'm not missing one bit. I guess I missed my calling back in the future. Yes, "McFly."

I love being in fresh, brisk air doing tasks that are stress-free, simple, and physically invigorating. The exercise is in the lifestyle. We are also in the process of digging a well—the "thinking about it" process. Did I say "we"?

I'm in better shape now than I've been since I was a child playing outside. In a way, it feels like playing all day with a good workout. I enjoy making things with my hands instead of working only with my brain as I did before. You know what I mean? Be it cooking homemade food, mending clothes, or tending vegetables, I'm learning so much! I feel so capable now.

Did you know that if you whip milk long enough you'll make whipped cream that, if you keep whipping, will become butter? I never knew that! Homemade butter is so creamy! I never loved butter as much as I do now.

The only problem has been the drought. The heat is so bad that we have to ration our water. The creek's gone low and is filling with sediment. Not tasting as good as it first did when I came here. We feed the cattle cactus stems to keep them hydrated. We've been eating them, too. Cactus soup is rather good, mind you.

Strangely, I'm not as hot as I was in "my time" when it got this hot. My loose, cotton blouse and billowy skirt keeps me feeling a lot cooler than the tight synthetic clothing I used to wear. It's almost like wearing a nightgown all day.

Sunday, June 3, 1877

The other night, walking back from the outhouse, I heard a big shuffle and saw a dark figure emerge. It was Sam.

"You all right?" I heard him ask before I could see his face in my lamp light.

"I had to pee."

My light hit his face. He was looking at me funny; I guess by the way I said it.

"Ouch!"

I had stepped on a sharp stone. I was shivering in my nightgown. I've no bathrobe. (Item number 2, cloth for bathrobe Sarah will help me make).

"Here," he reached out, "I'll carry you."

He picked me up and carried me back toward the house. He still smelled of sweat from the day's work.

"I didn't hear you take leave," he commented.

"I go out my window," I explained.

"You shouldn't much do that. Sometimes wolves will come down. That's why we keep the chickens and cow shut in at night."

"Wolves?" I shuddered. Not the coyotes I've seen but... wolves?

"Yep," he assured me.

So it's either get relief or get eaten! I NEED a CHAMBER POT!

Sam carried me all the way around the house to the front porch, set me down (drat), and opened the front door.

We said our good-nights before I scurried back into my bedroom and shut the door. Sigh!

3

A Strange Dream

Sunday, June 10, 1877

Last night, I dreamt a very strange dream. I dreamt that I was back where I came from at this state park called Paramount Ranch. It's an old studio lot that has Western town buildings still used for filming today, I mean, then. Later. Whatever! I used to take walks, jog, or picnic there a lot, living right nearby.

In this dream, it was night. I stood in the middle of the Western dirt street complete with mercantile, saloon, hotel, and a constable's station (they're not called sheriffs but constables in 1877). And a bank. Looks a lot like the little town of Barlow. Hmm. It was deserted. At the end of the main street is a lone train depot.

But in my dream there stood two men. They saw me and headed toward me. It was Sam and another man I'd never seen before. They looked confused. Lost? We were stuck in this place. A thick wall of fog surrounded the movie set town, surrounding hills and stream. Something told me we could not go into the fog. If we did, we would be lost forever.

We built a fire in the middle of the street and sat around it, at first in silence.

Neither man knew who I was. Even Sam had never met me before. He also seemed to not like or trust this other man. I could tell that Sam knew him somehow.

We had to sleep somewhere, and there was a hotel that had only two rooms: one upstairs and one downstairs. The stranger immediately took the room upstairs for himself. That left the room downstairs with one full bed and a fireplace for Sam and me. Sam begrudgingly insisted he sleep on the floor with a pillow and some blankets.

After nights of trying to convince him that I did not kick, drool, or bite, I was able to make him feel comfortable enough to take half the bed and then we slept with our backs to each other.

What a dream!

4

My Bright Idea

Tuesday, June 12, 1877

It's been especially hot. It must have been well over one hundred degrees today. I cannot tell you how refreshing the creek is. It somehow always stays cool. Perhaps the creek retains the earth's coldness from the night. No matter. I gulp it down like I used to do iced tea or smoothies in my time. It's weird how you change with your environment.

....

Wednesday, June 13, 1877

I was in the barn today, pouring buckets of milk into the butter churn, churning away, when Sam came in to get some rope. He had to reach over me to pull it off a nail. But he hovered there, like, I know it didn't take that long to remove it from the wall, y'know? I froze. Then he walked out.

Ugh! I really feel it now. And I wonder how much he does? If at all. I don't know if it's my imagination, but it feels like there is an unspoken connection between us. I dare not write further about this lest anyone should ever pry into here! I wish I had a lock for you, diary. I don't know what to do. But I feel I'm gonna have to do something.

Monday, June 25, 1877

The boys and I set off in the supply wagon today to get some, well, supplies: raw foodstuffs such as sugar, flour, salt for preserving the meat, as well as nails for Sam. But I had my own agenda. The boys have never been to school. They told me Barlow didn't have a school! Sarah had taught Gunnar to read and write.

I went to the mayor's office. The first thing he asks me is if I'm Sam's sister! He said I looked a little like Sam and so he thought I was visiting or something. But I assured him I was not and told him I wanted to inquire if they had schooling for the children. Or might they be planning to build a schoolhouse? And might they be in need of a teacher?

I had a BA in English and had done substitute teaching for a while when I thought about becoming a schoolteacher years ago.

Mayor Naylor said they were, in fact, opening a schoolhouse presently but they had already sent for a teacher from another town. But perhaps, sir, she may require an apprentice! Well, I was determined to be it!

Dinner that night was quiet. Sam glanced at me from time to time. I can never read his expressions. I wonder if everything I feel is just all in my own head. Maybe I have misinterpreted everything he's done.

Then Paul dropped his tin cup on the table and gleefully announced, "Renee called on the mayor today and has want to be a teacher!"

"Really?" Sarah asked, startled.

Sam just turned his ambiguous eyes onto me and asked, "Why that?"

"I just thought I should look into it," I explained, "I don't want to wear out my welcome here."

"You're not wearing your welcome, dear. You've been a blessing to us with all your labor." Sarah smiled.

I wanted to run right out of the house. I could just feel Sam staring at me.

"I thought you found us pleasin' to be around," I then heard him say.

"I do. Really, I do. I just didn't think you'd want me to be around this long," I surmised.

"We had not foreseen it," he went on, "but it seems to us, you are a fine fit for the ranch. Everythin's gettin' better with your added hand."

I grinned sheepishly and went on eating. No one had any more to say the rest of the meal.

However, Sarah was interested in how much I knew about teaching and if I might help young Paul learn how to read and count. Of course!

....

Friday, July 6, 1877

I've been here a few months now but still feel like a stranger. The Egans are very good to me, but sometimes I just feel lonely being the outsider who suddenly plopped into their lives.

Feliz has stopped needing milk and eats with Clover in the field now. Now there's something I never thought I'd have in my life—a pet lamb. She's more like my child, though, the way I treat her. 'Course I never thought I'd be living in the 1870s either. This is the longest dream I've ever had! I wish I could fly.

Well, Feliz has grown a lot, and her wool is coming in thick. But it will be a year before she can be sheared. Mrs. Townsend gave me a heap of wool from Feliz's mama to make yarn.

First, we gathered cochineal from the cactus plants to make red dye. Cochineals are bugs that hide in puffed, white cocoons affixed on cactus plants. When you squish them, a deep red goo oozes out. Indians use it to dye their blankets, clothing, teepees, and even to paint their horses, I hear.

Sarah has begun teaching me to spin the wool into yarn using a drop spindle, which is a wooden wand with a wooden disc at the bottom. You tie string around it in such a way that it spins by itself as you hold it by the hanging string. With your other hand, you attach a piece of shredded wool to the string. So while you spin the spindle, you keep adding wool until you get this string of yarn you can wrap around the wand. It's not easy, I'll tell ya that! This is one task I wish I could watch TV while I did it.

Late at night, when I can't sleep, I find my only comfort in my Bible. I have the Good News translation. I call mine Bible for dummies because it's in plain, modern English that I can understand. I ripped out and burned the copyright page indicating the publishing year, 1976, when I first got here. It was my sister's when she went to Mercy High School when we were growing up in Baltimore. Don't know how I ended up with it.

But every night I read some of it before bed. I look forward to it, like an old, familiar friend who is always there for me. The flame of my oil lamp brushes the pages of the Holy book with a fluttery glow and I take in God's Word.

Night magic, I used to call it as a kid. It's when the world has gone to sleep and it's only you and God in the complete stillness of the night. It's like you are suddenly in another sacred world separate from the jeering reality of daytime.

At night in my little room with my kindling lamp and dwindling fire in the small hearth, I am transported into this serenity. I feel God's "magic" all around me. Similar to the mystical feeling I'd get watching that scene in *Raiders of the Lost Ark* when Indiana Jones uses a staff and headpiece to pinpoint the location of the ark in the underground map room. Just John William's score alone for that scene is holy and haunting. That is the magical feeling of God's presence.

I am lulled to sleep by the soft chirping of crickets outside and, oftentimes, the soothing hoots of an owl—God's signal that it's time to go to sleep.

Tomorrow, I will awaken to the natural alarm of the rooster and cheerful chirps of birds. Even through His creatures, God calms our nights and brightens our mornings.

Sunday, August 19, 1877

We had a town picnic after church today. I was lying on a blanket staring up at a tall, lean Sycamore tree, watching its dainty green leaves sway in the wind.

Occasionally, strands of bark would break off exposing more of its white trunk. Little goldfinches hopped about the tree limbs chirping gregariously. Again, I say, how good God is to us to fill the world with both beautiful sights and sounds.

Sam and the boys were playing baseball with the other family men and boys. Sarah sat on a nearby blanket, chatting with other ladies. I lay there deep in thought about Sam. No, just utterly confused!

Here I am living in my dream world with my dream man, his wife and his children. I feel like I'm in heaven but just outside the pearly gates, looking in. And shame on me! When I should be focused on the Lord and want Him above anyone, especially Sam. That thought made me laugh.

Just then, a shadow fell over me, blocking the sun. Sam. Figures. He just looked at me. I really hated when he did that and loved it at the same time. Then he sits down next to me. Curious eyes of the women sitting with Sarah turned our way. Sarah paid them no mind.

"Enjoying yourself?" he asked me.

"Yes, quite," I replied.

"What are you looking at?" he inquired, squinting up at the tree.

"The goldfinches up there," I answered. "They're so cute."

"Cute," he tried out the word and looked full at me. Then he got up to get some water from a dipper and bucket. Oh, help me, Lord!

5

Odd Happenings

Tuesday, August 21, 1877

Today, when we took our monthly excursion to Barlow, something really odd happened. Sarah and I went into the general store whilst Sam and the boys called on the blacksmith (Smithy John, he's known as) to get some nails made.

We bought quite a bit, having not been to town in over a month. Mr. Kane, the owner of the mercantile, asked Sarah if I was Sam's sister! Agh! Why do people think this? I guess it's the only logical conclusion to my presence among the Egans.

As Mr. Kane added up our goods at the counter, Sarah pulled out the money she and Sam had saved.

But Mr. Kane held up his hand and said, "These groceries are paid for, ma'am. Put your money away."

Sarah was baffled. He told us she had a benefactor who wished to remain anonymous but insisted on paying for any goods she bought the next time she was in town. Mr. Kane said this benefactor (he wouldn't even indicate whether male or female) knew the Egans were having some hardship and just wished to do their Christian duty and help out where one could.

Well, it took Sarah several minutes of insisting to Mr. Kane that he take her money and return this mysterious charity to its generous owner. But, alas, she was forced to take the foodstuffs instead, debt free, because Mr. Kane refused to budge. He said he was under the strictest orders that he must abide.

When we walked out onto the dirt street, Sarah told me not to tell Sam or the boys because she was going to hide their grocery money for savings. Our secret! Shhh!

Saturday, August 25, 1877

I've taken notice that Sarah has been quieter since we learned of her mysterious benefactor. Well, tonight I learned something more. Sam turned in early, exhausted and achy from unloading wood he had chopped to build a fence around the barn (for Feliz—isn't that sweet?). So it was only Sarah and I at the hearth tonight.

She seemed lost in the fire when I asked her what was on her mind. She said she was just thinking about her mother and sisters back east. Then she started telling me all about them. I was astonished!

Sarah told me she had grown up in a prominent family—a few generations of owners of the North Bank of Boston. They were wealthy!

"A good Christian family with their hearts in the community" she said.

But only an adoring mother and two younger sisters remained.

Then her eyes grew solemn and more distant as she reminisced more. Sarah, just seventeen when the war broke out, met Sam at a social celebrating the newly enlisted Union soldiers. It was a chance for the boys in blue to have a last dance with the young ladies of society. Sam and Sarah immediately took to one another and talked like they'd known each other for years. It was hard for me to hear but hard not to, at the same time.

Sam told Sarah that his family had a small farm outside of Philadelphia in a small township called Hobbs Forge. He was one of two brothers going off to war (his younger brother, Joseph, was later killed in action at Manassas). The army paid well, and Sam's parents needed the extra income.

Sam's family was poor but not in a miserable way. They had each other and that was all they ever needed. Sarah fell in love with Sam the moment he said this. She knew right then, she told me, that this was the man she wanted to marry. I felt a twinge in my heart but tried not to show it.

Then two years later, a young businessman called at Sarah's manor while her family commenced high tea. He wanted to talk to her father (their surname was Gunnarsson). This young man, she recalled, was striking but had a shrewdness to him that made Sarah leery. He and her father spoke behind closed doors for some time before the young man left. He would look full at Sarah, and it gave her "the willies".

This gentleman returned, again and again, for dinners, Sunday picnics on the back lawn, and suppers. He seemed not to be able to stay away, and his increasing attention to Sarah made her increasingly uncomfortable.

But her father really took to the young man and seemed to encourage his admiration of Sarah, which she now abhorred.

Finally, the young man said he was going off for a while. Among her father's parting words to him was that Sarah would be waiting for him upon his return. Not on her life! She was so terrified that her father had it in his mind to marry her to this questionable sir, they had an argument.

Mr. Gunnarsson told his dutiful daughter that she could not marry Sam as she had hoped. Though well-liked Sam may be for his manner and values, he would most likely make her a poor widow with the death tolls so high, particularly at Gettysburg only a month before. So Sarah ran away and hid at the Egan farm until Sam returned from war. Fortunately, it was only three months before he did with a wounded leg he was unusually fortunate not to lose; a lead ball "merely broke his calf," as she put it.

The country reverend married them in the Egan home where Sam and Sarah remained for another year until Gunnar was born.

Then they learned about land being given away out west and set their hearts on claiming many acres to build a good life, unaware of the struggle and strife that lay ahead for them. They nearly starved the first few years out here and then Paul was born.

"But with God's help we have sustained," Sarah concluded with a sigh of contentment.

Of her own family, she said no more. Wow! I had no idea.

6

The Schoolmarm's Apprentice

Monday, August 27, 1877

Okay, I'm embarrassed. I couldn't stand my hairy legs and arm pits any longer. I haven't shaved since I've been here! I feel like Chewbacca! So I decided I was going to try to do something about it. But I had to time it right. When Sam and Sarah put the fire out in the living area and went to bed, I crept out the front door and grabbed Sam's razor off of the basin on the porch.

So, I'm in my room in my nightgown with my bare leg mounted upon the windowsill, trying ever so carefully to shave my leg without cutting myself when my bedroom door flies open and there's Sam! He's staring at my naked leg. A strong feeling of attraction shot right through me. I put my leg down and my nightgown draped over it.

"What are you doing?" He demanded to know. "Is that my razor?"

"Yes, sir," I answered apologetically.

He came over and grabbed it off the sill.

"What were you doing?" he demanded to know.

"I was shaving my legs," I stammered.

He just looked appalled.

"Why?" he exclaimed.

Now I was appalled.

"Why?" I squealed.

"Go to sleep," he ordered.

But he stopped at the door and shook his razor dry, frowning at me.

"I bes' never catch you with my razor again, you here?"

"Yes, sir." I nodded. I guess hairy's in!

Wednesday, August 29, 1877

Well! We've had enough hearing about John Wesley Hardin! Gunnar has been talking for days about the news he heard in town when he and Sam went to Smithy John's to get some hooks made to suspend the lanterns in the kitchen.

At dinner, Gunnar explained all about the notorious outlaw who was arrested last Friday. Gunnar said Hardin sewed pockets in his vest in such a way that he could cross his arms and draw his pistols quickly. This John Wesley Hardin was using a false name, James W. Swain, when he was knocked out by rangers on a train in Pensacola, Florida only because his guns got caught in his suspenders and could not draw in time.

He allegedly killed twenty-seven men total, although the *Weekly Arizona Miner* (according to Postman Wickerman who read it to Gunnar) states that Hardin claims he actually killed forty-two men.

"Hardin killed all those men because, as he said, 'I take no sass but 'sasparilla' (he means sarsaparilla)," Gunnar reported with unenviable enthusiasm.

I'm gonna remember that one! Sam then enlightened Gunnar with the likelihood of this man being sentenced to hang.

Finally, Sarah had enough because it was beginning to arouse Paul's interest and ordered Gunnar to "cease speaking any further about this unseemly man."

I wish she had just stopped at "cease speaking any further"!

Saturday, September 1, 1877

Guess what? I was hired by Mayor Naylor as a schoolmarm's apprentice! Yeay! I'm to be paid twenty-five cents a day! That's like twenty-two dollars a day in my time. Well, it's something. I start Monday. Gunnar and Paul are also attending this all-grades-in-one-room schoolhouse. This should be interesting.

Friday, September 7, 1877

My first week at school has ended. The students are quite behaved, so it seems this will be easier than anticipated; although, they look a little afraid. The schoolteacher is a woman who looks to be in her late forties (watch she's probably younger than me, right?) named Ms. Schumacher. She is a tall, spindly woman with a tight bun and rectangular spectacles that usually hang low on her long, thin nose. She is pleasant enough. Rather stern, though.

Paul likes that I'm there, but Gunnar can't stand it, especially when I get to order him around, like, to go to the chalkboard to add sums. Heh-heh. I try to give him the difficult ones. Maybe I will earn his respect here.

Friday, September 14, 1877

Ms. Schumacher. What else can I say about her? I have yet to see her smile. Or laugh. I can't imagine going through life never smiling or laughing. I laugh at the drop of a hat.

She doesn't like me; I can just tell. You know when you can just tell someone you barely know doesn't like you? She also asked me if I was Sam's sister! STOP, PEOPLE!

For starts, she didn't want an apprentice. And it's becoming apparent after only two weeks of working with her that nothing I do is satisfactory to her.

My ideas, innovative as they are, are a bit too modern and not well received. For instance, I thought it would be a novel idea to have science be a part of the pupils' studies and that we could begin with a little biology. Have the children gather things of nature that intrigue them: rocks, leaves, dead insects, moss, flowers, what have you. And we could buy a magnifying glass by which they could view their specimen and write down what they observe about them. Then we could learn some facts about the natural specimen's physiology that are in books these days.

Well, she doesn't like this idea one bit. She thinks it's "too imaginative." Like that's a bad thing!

Wednesday, September 19, 1877

Well, I never! She fired me! Excuse me, she "released me" was how she put it. That spinster! (Okay, look who's talking, Miss Over-Forty-Myself who's never been married.) But still! She's a witch! According to Mayor Naylor, Ms. Schumacher told him that I was of no use to the schoolhouse. In fact, I was a "hindrance" in her words.

It really hurts me on a lot of levels. I really tried to do well and I thought my modern ideas would have really enriched the town's children and even help them aspire to be more than what they may end up being with the standard expectations of these times. Who knows what they could achieve and what impact it would have on their lives and the future as a whole!

Maybe that's a bit grandiose to think all that could come from the influences of a schoolmarm's apprentice, but I so wanted to do as much as I could for these kids.

For me, too, it was a sense of relief to be away daily from the ranch, to get away from Sam for a while so I could work on getting over him. And the money I made was such a blessing to the Egans. Almost overnight, we were able to buy all the things sorely overdue on our list, including cloth for my bathrobe and chamber pot. Now I won't have to go outside, freezing and risking getting eaten by wolves to go to the bathroom at night! Just have to make sure I don't step in a pot of pee every morning.

Life on the Egan ranch had improved considerably. Sam was already talking about the prospect of hiring a vaquero (ranch hand) or two. And then, just like that, it was all taken away. For no good reason but that I was too imaginative.

Now we struggle again. Sadly, we hadn't even begun to save because we figured my first month's pay would get the things we so badly needed and then we could begin saving. It's been dismal at the house for a week now.

The boys had to drop out of school completely; well, they can go in, like, once a week to get some lessons. But Sam needs them on the ranch every day now since he's not gonna be able to hire vaqueros.

So I help the boys at night after supper for an hour with reading, writing, and arithmetic. See if I don't teach them better than ol' Ms. Schumacher after all! Maybe they're better off. Let's hope so.

Ms. S even complained to Sarah about the boys not being in school now! But who fired whom and consequently made all this happen? Okay, I'm not naming names. Am I still sore? I think this bothers me more, that the boys have to miss school now, than the mere fact of being fired when I was only trying to help.

And, on top of it all, I'm having a hard time dealing with my emotions regarding Sam. I realize how badly I missed him every day and I've been barely able to conceal the exhilaration that wells up inside me every time I see him now. Dang her! I wish I knew what Sam thought about me.

I thought this apprenticeship was the perfect solution to it all. See, I would have been able to get some money saved up to get my own little place in town. I would be independent while still being able to help Sam and Sarah out financially. I really need to get away from him, though I can't bear to.

If only Mayor Naylor knew the impact he had on our lives by listening to that prig, Ms. S! He gave us the rug and then pulled it out from under us. Okay, enough of blaming other people for my troubles. I guess I'm as much to blame for being too imaginative.

Okay, stop!

Saturday, September 22, 1877

Oh, my goodness! A frightful but rather funny thing happened today. I decided to go fishing by myself this afternoon. I just needed to be alone for a while to think things through and get a hold over my emotions. So there I sat by the big creek on the edge of the Egan's land with my fishing line cast out, when I saw a bear across the creek. I froze. He crawled into the water and started right toward me!

Hardly aware of what I was doing, I stood up and yanked my line out of the creek, which was tugging and—would you believe—had a big, fat trout on the hook! The biggest I ever caught! Well, I ran with the pole over my shoulder dragging the fish on the ground behind me, screaming. That bear chased me, trying to grab the fish! I ran in circles, I think, 'cause the bear was turning in circles trying to grab it.

Finally, I gathered my wits and dropped the fishing pole. As the bear ate my prize fish, I walked away on shaky legs distant enough from the bear that, upon finishing his meal, retreated across the creek. He barked back at me as if with thanks.

Sarah said I was as white as a ghost when I walked in the front door. When I told them the story, they all laughed hysterically; although, they were relieved for my safe escape. Except Gunnar says he doesn't believe a word of it, especially about me catching a prize-sized fish. Boys!

7

A Stranger in Town

Saturday, September 22, 1877

I suppose I should mention the man who has come to town. What's really weird and freaks me out is that he looks like the man who appeared in that dream I had about being with Sam and the stranger at Paramount Ranch. I can't believe I never wrote about this earlier. Ms. S had me so stressed out, I never got to it.

It's spooky to have dreamt about someone and then meet them in real life. If this is real life.

At any rate, this man showed up at school one day when I was still the schoolmarm's apprentice. He just walked into the schoolhouse in the middle of the day. All heads turned around to look at him. I immediately recognized him from my dream. It was spooky!

Well, he tipped his black bowler hat to Ms. S and gave me a queer appraisal that put a shiver down my spine. Then he sat down on a back bench next to one of our older students, Howard, a boy of sixteen.

Though he was finely dressed in a black suit with a Western bow tie and had a round, handsome face, he had a cagey demeanor that warned you he may be up to something.

"What are we learning today?" the stranger wanted to know.

Ms. Schumacher was speechless, as were I and all the children. Then the mistress found her voice and asked the stranger what he was doing here. He replied he wanted to learn like all the rest of the pupils. She told him to leave, that his presence was inappropriate. At which he responded he would leave upon learning something.

He wore a pistol, so Ms. Schumacher was obliged to go on teaching. As she talked nervously about vowels, nouns, and consonants, I noticed the man began scribbling on a piece of paper with Howard's pencil.

Then he dropped both pencil and paper on the long desk (making everyone shudder), got up, and walked out of the schoolhouse without another word.

Howard picked up the paper and gave it to me. I just stared at it. Ms. Schumacher pestered me to see what the man wrote down. When I showed it to her, she just pursed her lips. It was a beautiful, well-drawn sketch of me! And he signed it "Jethro Mason."

As soon as we left the schoolhouse, Paul shouted that he was going to tell Pa about the stranger. Apparently, they knew who he was! Gunnar was less inclined to tell Pa, I mean, Sam! But neither one of those stinkers would tell me why! They were too excited and ran ahead of me.

"Pa! Guess who came into school today?" Paul screamed, running into the house.

"Paul, soften your voice, please," Sarah scolded him.

Sam looked up from the fireplace where he was pouring coffee from the tin coffee pot.

"Who, son?"

"Don't say it," Gunnar warned Paul.

"You won't believe it, Pa!" Paul jumped about.

"Bes' shut it," Gunnar further forewarned.

"No?" Sam raised a brow, his interest piqued. "Why, who, son?"

"Why, Jethro Mason!" Paul said with mischievous eyes.

Sam just stared at the child, speechless.

"What?" he eventually muttered.

"I told ya to say nil!" Gunnar reprimanded his brother.

"It's the truth, Pa," Paul went on, excitedly. "He sat in the rear and drew a portrait of Renee. Is he not the awful man from Boston who caused injury to dear Morfar Gunnarsson, Pa?"

I stopped dead in my tracks. What? Sam was now lost in the fire.

"Boys, wash for supper," Sarah urged them with a quiver in her voice.

Sam pulled me aside, concerned about what had transpired in school that day. But I could tell him no more than Paul had. I wanted so bad to ask him who this man was and what he had done. I wanted to tell him about my dream too, but I just couldn't find the courage.

Supper was quiet that night. No one mustered up anything to say. Sarah sent the boys to bed early, and we sat around the fire—just Sam, herself, and I. Sarah opened her Bible and read Proverbs 3:5–7 (KJV).

> "Trust in the Lord with all thine heart; and lean not unto thine own understanding. In all thy ways acknowledge Him, and He shall direct thy paths. Be not wise in thine own eyes: fear the Lord, and depart from evil."

Trust in the Lord. Do you realize that we trust God a lot more than we realize we do? Even those who don't believe in God trust Him, whether they realize it or not. I'll prove it. And then I gotta hit the hay.

When you wake up each morning, do you worry your heart may not beat? Do you worry that gravity might suddenly disappear and you'll go floating up into space? Do you worry that the ground won't be there to walk on? Or that dinosaurs might evolve back into the food chain and eat you for dinner? No, you don't. (At least, I hope not!) And why don't you worry about these things? Enough said.

We sound like clay pots when we question God. Dagnabbit, where is it? Here:

> "Does a clay pot dare argue with its maker, a pot that is like all the others? Does the clay ask the potter what he is doing? Does the pot complain that its maker has no skill?" (Isaiah 45:9 GNT)

Goodnight, to whoever I'm talking to. I guess it's you, diary. My, aren't we contentious tonight! Okay, this is scary. Goodnight.

....

Sunday, September 30, 1877

It is uncertain to everyone what this man, Jethro Mason, is doing in town but there's been a lot of murmuring amongst folk in the mercantile, at the post office, and after church.

'Course, ever since construction of railroad tracks have commenced on the perimeter of the Egan ranch, through town and beyond, there's been constant talk in the township especially at the Sunday picnics, which Sarah reproves as beastly to discuss such industrial matters on the Sabbath. I have to agree that it's more honorable to God to keep His holy day holy.

I have to say, I've found people here to be much more respectful of God's commands than where I come from. Here, people seem to be conscientious that the life hereafter far outweighs the one they are living now.

That's the *big* difference. I couldn't place my finger on it. People in this place and time (the majority) speak and act as though they live for God rather than for themselves. Much of them put God first in their homes, their family, in every decision they make, what have you. Businesses are closed on Sundays, as they were when I was a child in the 20ᵗʰ century. Good grief, that makes me feel old. I never thought the day would come when businesses would be open on Sundays.

And most of the people (here in 1877) know God's Word! That's where their strength comes from. When you are in great distress and can recall, off the top of your head, a passage like the one on my bookmarker, Isaiah 41:10 (msg):

> Don't panic. [Clearly one for me!] I'm with you. There's no need to fear for I'm your God. I'll give you strength. I'll help you. I'll hold you steady, keep a firm grip on you.

When you can summon that up in a dreadful moment, you've got some invincible arsenal against worry and fear!

People of the nineteenth century (generally) are very humble and hard working, too. They think in terms of a group, a family, a community rather than as an individual. What is best for my family? What is best for my church? My town?

They also have such tremendous appreciation for every little thing they have. Nothing they possess is ever considered trivial. The things they own are for practical use in their daily lives. Very little (if anything) is acquired for decoration or amusement. And they don't possess much. Homes are pretty bare around here.

And you know what? These people don't need Prozac! They are very content, very in acceptance of their circumstances and what they have to deal with, or overcome, to live. Be it drought, illness, poverty, family separation, whatever crisis they face, you rarely hear anyone complain. Tolerant! That's the word I was looking for. They are very tolerant of life's challenges. You know what I mean? But let's not make them out to be saints. There are certainly other things that they do not tolerate (things of which we twenty-first century folk can commend ourselves for being so), to be sure. But I digress.

As per Galatians 5:22–23 (GNT), "But the Spirit produces love, joy, peace, patience, kindness, goodness, faithfulness, humility, and self-control. There is no law against such things as these."

That's the creed these people live by, by their very nature because of the Spirit within them. I have to say, aside from the John Wesley Hardins, who kill people for snoring, I am very impressed with most folks here in 1877.

Wednesday, October 3, 1877

We went to Barlow today to get more flour, salt, and lard. There is a mysterious large building being built in the middle of town, and no one seems to know what it is except for the mayor and Constable Dunn, who are keeping it under their hats. But it is a "monstrosity" (I've heard it called) constructed of, not wood, but brick and concrete. And several stories high!

Talking to Mrs. Kane in the general store, we learned that the mayor will announce it at the town dance this Friday night. There will be free punch and cake! Woo-hoo! I'm so excited! I don't know when was the last time I had cake! Not since I've been here. Cake is not something for which we've had the luxury to buy sugar for in the Egan household.

And I can't remember the last time I've been dancing!

Friday, October 5, 1877

Sarah taught me how to curl my hair for the dance by tying strips of cloth to the ends of my hair that I then rolled up tight and tied again close to my scalp. I slept on it and awoke with dry, curly hair. Very curly. My curling iron, back in my day, would not compare.

8

The Town Dance

Friday, October 5–Saturday, October 6, 1877

Oh, boy. I don't know where to begin. I'm still shaking. But I must get this out of my system so I can calm down enough to go to sleep. It must be close to (or after) midnight and we get up at the crack of dawn.

Okay, why don't I start with the dance. It was enchanting, held in the mill warehouse. Barrels lined the walls. People sat on them or tabled their jugs, tin cups, and tea cups on them.

Decorative Chinese lanterns flickered with a warm glow above the crowd as a string quartet played chipper tunes. Many folks were lined up in facing rows to dance a delightful contra dance called the Virginia Reel that commenced as we walked in. Sarah tapped me excitedly; this was the song she kept telling me she hoped to hear. It reminded me of square dancing, a little.

At first, the Egans and I just watched. The boys looked like they'd never seen dancing before. I wanted to dance so badly but there was only one man I wanted to dance with, and he stood beside his wife standing beside me taking the whole scene in. I suppose it had been awhile for them too, dancing. It hurt. It stung.

And then, what stung me more, Sam held out his hand to Sarah and they moved onto the dance floor to join in. My heart sunk to my feet. I know it should not have, yet it did. I couldn't move or remove my eyes from them dancing, smiling into each other's eyes.

Sarah was wearing a gorgeous pale-blue silk dress trimmed in white lace she had pulled from her trunk. She was beautiful! It was the dress she wore (and not since) the night she met Sam at the Union social. It was tucked away all these years at the foot of their bed for the next occasion when she might dance again. Sarah was elated that it still fit.

And my gown! Sarah surprised me with it earlier today. She made it for me. The skirt is a merlot-shade floral-print and the top is a matching, V-shaped bodice with billowy short sleeves and burgundy silk trim. It's so lovely!

She made it so that I would have a nice dress to wear for such an occasion as this. I cried when she gave it to me. So much work went into it, and I know not when she did it! She said since she didn't know when was my birthday, she thought this was as good a time as any to give it to me. As much as I hurt over Sam, I love and adore Sarah. She has a pure heart. She is a true friend.

Overwhelmed, I had to leave Paul and Gunnar to go outside because I was couldn't help but cry. The boys were too distracted by the goings-on to notice my departure anyway. Then I bumped into a broad man coming in. It was the stranger from the schoolhouse and my dream—Mr. Jethro Mason himself.

"Well, hello, again," he greeted me.

Don't ask me to dance, my brain barked.

It was typical in my past (such as at high school dances) that I always stood on the side, watching the one I favored dance with his girlfriend. And it never failed that some unwanted, poor soul would approach me, completely unaware of the distress I showed watching the one I really wanted to dance with. Wasn't it ever obvious that I did not want to dance with someone else at that moment?

For the first time, it was. Jethro was different. He studied my expression and took it very much into consideration before he spoke again.

"You look like you might benefit from a glass of punch. I hear it's pretty good, if you catch my meaning." He winked, making me giggle. "Would you care for some?"

"Sure," was all I could respond.

I know I should have said, "Yes, thank you, dear, sir," but he appeared undisturbed by my crude reply.

Anything to get me away from my view of Sam and Sarah! We gently pushed our way through the crowded mill to the display of refreshments. Oh my! There were rum cake, pies, and puddings served on china with real silver cutlery and a big crystal bowl of punch.

"You've taken residence at the Egan's ranch, haven't you?" Jethro asked, handing me a crystal tea cup of punch.

"Yes," I answered, carefully. How did he know that?

"Are you Sam Egan's sister?"

Why does everybody keep asking that? The whole town believes I'm Sam's sister! I must be, they say. What with the same high cheek bones and auburn hair. And there's been several times when Sam almost said I was! Bugger!

"No!" I screeched without restraint. "I AM NOT SAM'S SISTER!"

It quite amused him, my exasperation.

"You're Jethro Mason, aren't you, sir?" I asked him. Let's move the conversation on!

"Yes, I am. And I don't have the privilege of knowing your name, young lady."

"Renee. Twining."

I was never sure how much to reveal lest it prompt more problematic questions. I could tell by Jethro Mason's expression his mind was wheeling in attempts to come to some explanation for my presence among the Egans.

"You're no longer serving as apprentice at the schoolhouse, I hear," he probed.

"No, sir, I was terminated."

He grinned. "I'm sorry to hear that. Personally, I think your idea for science lessons was a good one."

This confounded me.

"How did you know about that, sir?"

"Mayor told me," Mason explained. "So, what are you doing at the Egan ranch?"

The Virginia Reel had ended. Sam and Sarah rejoined the boys. Sam was looking for me. But the mayor had taken the platform at the far end of the warehouse and was clanging his glass with a spoon for everyone's attention.

The town's people moved in tighter, blocking me from Sam's view.

"I would like to make an announcement," Mayor Naylor exclaimed. "You are all well aware that we have a new building bein' built in town, quite a large one. Folks have inquired with me about it on many occasions. Well, I am now at liberty to disclose this secret to you all."

Everyone seemed to hold their breath. Jethro turned around with his arms crossed as though to hide himself.

The mayor continued, "We are building a *ho*tel!"

Gasps lifted from the warehouse with cheers and applause.

"You all know that the railroad is upon the threshold of our town to extend all the way through the whole state of Arizona. This new *ho*tel will make our town an appealin' railroad stop for travelers coming to and from California. With travelers stayin' at our new hotel, this will bring in more revenue and business for our town's merchants!"

A roar of approval drowned him out.

"That's right," the mayor shouted. "And we owe this to our latest visitor who has generously built one of his Pristine *Ho*tels right here in Barlow to make all this possible. Mr. Jethro Mason! Mr. Mason, come up here and say hello to our townsfolk. C'mon, now."

Begrudgingly, our generous benefactor excused himself from me and waded through the applauding crowd, up to the mayor's side where he took a weak bow. I could see Sam now. He was glaring at Jethro like something awful. I've never seen his face so severe. Sarah's face was hidden by her fan.

"Thank you," Jethro said, looking timid for the first time I ever seen. "Thank you all."

He made a quick bow before disappearing into the crowd applauding him again.

Another song began with a joyful twang. Folks lined up to dance a quadrille (done with four couples in square formation). Sarah coaxed Sam back on the dance floor, I suspect partly to deter him from concerning himself with Jethro. What did this man do?

Watching Sam and Sarah dance again, it became apparent to me just how much they really loved each other. I couldn't help my tears from streaming again. I tried to hide my face but no one paid me any mind anyway. So I thought. Before I knew it, Jethro Mason was back before me.

"Now, that ain't right. A pretty, little thing like you crying," he placated me.

But I couldn't stop.

"Here," Jethro offered me a handkerchief. "How ' about we waltz out of here and over to my new hotel. It would delight me to show you its décor on the inside. I could benefit highly from the opinion of the fairer sex.

"I'd love to," I decided. I took his arm and out the mill we strolled.

Mr. Mason led me across the empty dirt street to his fancy hotel lit from inside lamps. Its glass door was etched with its name: PRISTINE HOTEL OF BARLOW. He unlocked it, and we went inside.

Wow, inside was so plush and polished.

It had scarlet curtains that perfectly matched the carpet and velvet-cushioned sofas and chairs that looked right out of Ethan Allen. It was like walking out of dusty Barlow and into nineteenth century New York City!

Jethro lit another few lamps and raised his arms up at his grand hotel (that also contained a saloon, of course).

"So tell me, do you find it agreeable?"

"It's absolutely beautiful!" I exclaimed.

"Thank you kindly. I chose the décor myself. A lot went into building this place. Quite a lot."

I caught the emphasis in his last phrase.

"Mr. Mason?"

"Call me Jethro, darlin'."

"But that wouldn't be proper, sir," I duly noted. However, his curious expression changed my mind. "All right, Jethro, may I ask you a personal question?"

He considered me before answering, "Go ahead."

"How do you know Sam Egan?"

I couldn't help it; I had to know! I had to know why Sam distained the sight of him.

"I don't," was his answer.

Not the one I was expecting.

"Why?" Jethro continued, closing in on me. "Has he said something to you?"

"He hasn't said anything to me about you. But he always looks distressed when your name is brought up."

Jethro cracked a quick smile. "Is that right? Well, I have a question for you, too, and I would thank you for your honesty."

What did I have to be honest about?

"All right," I agreed.

Sternly, Jethro worded, "Now, Ms. Twining, explain to me why you are living with the Egans if you are of no relation to Sam. Nor of Sarah's, I presume?"

My mind reeled for an acceptable yet unrevealing answer.

"Let's just say," I thought aloud, "I came to be with them by circumstances, most of which I don't fully understand yet."

Oh, that was good! I could tell by the look on his face it wasn't the answer he was hoping for either. Then he bore a disturbing expression that told me he knew better and was not to be taken for a fool.

"We'll touch on that subject at a latter time," he concluded the matter. "I wonder, if Sam realizes…"

I could scarcely breathe; he was so intimidating.

"What?" I squeaked.

He was staring down at me with a cocked head like a predator sizing up its prey. Then he struck.

"How much attention you pay him," he finished.

"I-I don't know what you mean, s-sir," I stuttered. And, really, I didn't want to know either.

I should have left the hotel right then and there. If I had, perhaps everything thereafter would have turned out differently. Then I could sleep tonight instead of writing twenty-some pages in my diary!

"I've seen the way you look at him, like the way you were looking at him in the millhouse tonight while he was dancing with his wife. You fancy him, young lady. You fancy him a lot. I'd even venture to say that you might find yourself falling in love with him."

How dare he! It was more than I could bear. And from a stranger! Beastly. I edged for the door but he stopped me there.

"I don't mean to upset you, miss. I only desire to offer you some comfort and understanding. I supposed you could use some."

And darn it if my eyes didn't well up again! Dang glands! Next thing I knew I was burying my face in his coat as he patted my back. Finally, someone I could talk to about what has been pent up so deep for so long inside me—my secret sin. But did it have to be a man? And one Sam hated?

"Also," Jethro continued, "I wanted to offer you a way out."

"A way out?" I repeated, wiping my eyes dry.

Jethro got out his handkerchief and started drying my cheeks.

"I reckon you would feel a whole lot better if you weren't face to face with Sam and Sarah every day. What if you could remove yourself from them for a while?"

"What do you mean, sir?"

"I mean, come work for me. Here at the hotel. I could use another girl in the saloon. You'd make good money here. The men tip well in these parts to pretty ladies like yourself. You could live here. I'll give you your own room in the hotel."

"I don't know, Mr. Mason," I stammered. "It's awful kind of you but I don't know if they would want me to go just yet. With the ranch growing and—"

9

Truth Be Told

"Renee!"

I spun around and nearly hit Sam barging in. He was fuming. Without another word, he grabbed me and pulled me out the door.

"Just having a nice conversation here, Sam. No need to wrangle the lady," I heard Jethro say before we were in the street.

I could see Mr. Mason silhouetted in the front doorway as Sam dragged me down the street.

Sam's grip was hurting me but he wouldn't say a word, and I was afraid to. The mill was dark! The dance had long since ended and the last of the crowd were dwindling out. Sarah and the boys were nowhere in sight, and I was afraid to ask how they might of gotten off because the Egans' wagon was still there. Sam pushed me up on the buckboard and whipped Mazy into action.

The ride home was silent at first. I kept my eyes on the multitude of stars that I get lost in every night. I still can't get over how many there are! Sam broke my trance, speaking at last.

"What in tarnation possessed you to take leave with him like that? Did I not forbid you to ever speak with this man?

No, not really. I guess he figured I'd never have the opportunity.

"What happened between you and him?" I retorted.

"That's none of your affair, and you are to never ask me that again. And never ever speak to him again! You hear? If I ever catch you talking to that man once more, I will throw you out of my house! You got that?"

Got it! But I wasn't through.

"Mr. Mason, offered me a job at the hotel."

The saloon was part of the hotel, right?

"I could make good money," I continued, "and help you buy more feed and more of everything. It would help."

"You're not working for him. Do you know what he's offering? For you to be a whore in a whorehouse. That's his meaning of a job. You are to never go near him again. Just shut up about it," he growled.

That was all I could take. About to leap out of my skin, I jumped off the wagon. Sam was livid as he pulled Mazy to a halt. I was already heading back toward town on foot, but he caught me and whipped me back around.

"I have to leave you all!" I cried.

"What do you mean, leave?" he yelled.

"I have to get away from you!"

"Why?"

"Because I can't bear to look at you anymore! I just…you have to let me go!"

I pulled away from him, but he wouldn't let go.

"Tell me what's bothering you," he demanded.

"Let me go! I cried.

I managed to tear away and ran. I just ran. But he caught up to me in no time and held on to me tightly.

"What is the matter with you?" He was in my face.

"I just can't live with you anymore," I sobbed.

"Why?"

"Because I can't take it anymore!"

"What can't you take?" he prodded me.

"What I feel for you."

Like a caged bird suddenly released it just flew out of my mouth. Sam grew silent and stared at me, digesting what he heard I guess.

He let me go. To my dismay, I bawled like a baby. Gently, he embraced me and I cried in his arms.

When we reached home, the fireplace flickered through the front windows. Sarah was up, mending one of Paul's shirts. It had to have been close to midnight. She stood up with worry, but Sam motioned to her not to speak.

I'm exhausted. I must go to sleep. G'night. Good grief.

Sunday, October 7, 1877

My confession—I cannot believe I made to Sam last night—fills me with agitation. Tonight, I read this in my Bible:

> A woman who had suffered from severe bleeding for twelve years came up behind Jesus and touched the edge of His cloak. She said to herself, "If only I touch His cloak, I will get well." Jesus turned around and saw her, and said, "Courage, my daughter! Your faith has made you well." At that very moment, the woman became well. (Matt. 9:20–22, GNT)

If only I could be healed of Sam. He's such a disease.

Monday, October 8, 1877

Last night, I was delightfully surprised by a pleasant and most amazing dream! And it wasn't about Sam and Jethro Mason this time. It was something completely new and refreshing.

I had often wondered what it would feel like to be face to face with Jesus if He still lived in the flesh among us. Can you imagine? Well, I got to experience it in this dream.

He was walking through a crowd of people, in His day and age. Except I was there only observing. Or so I thought. He was right in front of me. I just had to reach out and touch Him; I mean, who couldn't resist? I could feel His cloak in my hand, and something went through me like a force. It's the only way I can describe it.

Jesus turned around and surveyed me with His eyes as no one can. Wow! His eyes are so piercing. They touch your soul immediately. An instant serenity came over me like I'd never felt before.

He said to me, "You must be one of my disciples."

I looked around to see if He was speaking to someone else. Me? Little ol' me? He couldn't mean me. I felt so ashamed, thinking of all the sins I committed. Thinking of how I was so glued to Sam.

He read me clearly. "What makes you doubt what I say?"

I near whispered, "My sins, Lord. I'm wondering how I will ever be able to overcome all the evil temptations in my life."

Jesus leaned into me and looked me squarely in the eyes—so mesmerizing His were and so loving and understanding at the same time.

"You can't," He confirmed.

But then I smiled, knowing full well what He meant.

"I can't," I contemplated, "without you."

He smiled, happy I understood. "That's right."

Relieved and light-footedly, I walked on with Him through the crowd, without another concern.

Hmm, that reminds me of another passage. Where is it?

The Sovereign LORD gives me strength. He makes me sure-footed as a deer and keeps me safe on the mountains. (Hab. 3:19, GNT)

10

Sits with Bear

Saturday, October 13, 1877
Distressed. I'm all distress!

Sam came into the barn this morning when I was milking Clover. I nearly jumped when I heard his boots scuff in. I felt his eyes on me without even turning around. We've hardly said a word to each other since the night of the dance. He was at Thunder's stall behind me. Gunnar's black-and-white patched horse gurgled him a soft "mornin'."

Then Clover turned her head and mooed at me, scaring me half to death. I had stopped milking.

"When you're done with that, go help Sarah with breakfast." I heard him say.

I nearly fell of the milk stool. Okay, I normally help her with breakfast but was he just giving his regular orders? Or did she want to talk to me? I felt like I was walking to the gallows as I headed back to the house.

Thank goodness Sarah didn't want to "talk." But I noticed she was particularly quiet, too. I cannot tell you how uncomfortable I am right now.

Sam just left. He just came in to put more wood on my all-but-extinguished fire. But he wants me to put out the lamp soon. I told him just fifteen more minutes. He's gone now. He is really acting different. I should never have expressed my feelings to him. Now I can't take it back, and it's changed everything.

Sarah knows something's up; she's not naive. Sometimes I think she has ESP. She must know what I feel for her husband.

I want things to go back to the way they were. I want to rewind to Friday night and keep my mouth shut the whole ride home. No, I want to have never gone into that blasted hotel with Jethro!

Oh, shoot! *Jethro* knows. Would he ever say anything to anyone? What if the whole town of Barlow finds out I fancy Sam? Agh!

"Snuff out the lamp."

Sam just came in again. Guess I'm saying goodnight. G'night!

....

Wednesday, October 17, 1877

You won't believe what happened today! I got away a little this afternoon, finally, to go fishing. I had to be alone for a while and been waiting all week for this chance.

Despite how remorseful I felt, I was actually doing quite well. I caught five good-sized trout. But I needed to think. To cry. And I did just that. I buried my head in my arms and let it all out.

My own real family back east (in my time) have also been on my mind lately. It pains me not knowing if I'll ever see them again. I'd never felt as alone as I did this day.

I began to talk to the Lord. If I could only see Him. I told Him about everything, including how ashamed I've been of being so obsessed with Sam. Who was I kidding? I really had no intentions of getting over him. Sam was all that motivated me in life now, not God. I was breaking *the* first commandment: "Worship no god but Me" (Exod. 20:3, GNT).

Okay, like, I cringe to think of Sam as a god but that's exactly what he's become to me! An obsession with someone or something is the same as worshipping them. Someone once told me, "If it's what you're living for, it's what you worship."

I realized right then what was missing most from my life: a relationship with God, with Jesus.

Sure I accept Jesus Christ as my Savior (the first and most crucial step) and read my Bible daily. Sure I go to church and have been baptized. All of that facilitates the growth of a relationship with the Lord. And I can't tell you how good it feels when I'm in the Word. As well as how comforting it is to have a good fellowship with other believers.

But did I really have a relationship with Jesus or was I just going to Him only when I needed help? I'm sure He's like,

"Thanks, Renee." That's not a relationship! That's 911! Hm, haven't thought about my phone in a while.

Anyway, I wanted the Lord now more than ever. I wanted our relationship to be what He had intended it to be with humans from the get go when He was in the garden with Adam and Eve: a one-on-one relationship with God, the Creator of the universe! Who would give that up? What were they thinking!

But why do we give Adam and Eve such a bad rap? Who are we to judge them? If that forbidden tree had been made entirely of chocolate, I would have been in big trouble, if it had been me! I wouldn't have even needed Satan to tempt me. I would have been like, "Out of the way, snake! That tree is mine!" I wouldn't have just eaten the fruit; I would have eaten the whole dang tree! Even the roots. God would've come down and been like, "Where's My tree?" I wouldn't have shared any with Adam either. Man would've been off the hook. Good grief.

Oh, I want to have that kind of relationship with the Lord more than anything now! I want God beside me every day, all the way! Especially with there being chocolate and Sam in the world.

Imagine always having with you the One who created you! Who knows and understands you better than anyone, even yourself! The One who can help you make the right decisions and give you the courage to go through with them. The One who can make things happen in ways no one else can. Who can fill your heart when you are lonely...

What was that scripture Sarah read just tonight that warmed my heart so? Here it is in my Bible:

> Yet I always stay close to You, and You hold me by the hand. (Ps. 73:23, GNT)

"Oh, Lord, I need you!" I cried aloud over the creek.

Sunlight glittered on the rippling water as though reflecting His glory.

Then I heard a big splash! A bear! Now? He waded into the water, bobbing his head, up and down. Was it the same one as before? I could only hope because he started across the strong current toward me! Fear paralyzed me instantly. Now I knew what it meant to be scared stiff. I literally could not move to save my life; my muscles had locked.

The bear emerged onto the bank I sat on and towered over me on all fours. His shadow fell upon me, and I could feel his heavy panting.

But he was only interested in one thing: my basket full of fish. He looked at me as if to say, "You gonna eat these?" Then he proceeded to grab one with his gigantic teeth and laid it in front of himself like a chew bone. He just sat there next to me like a big dog eating his treat.

I could only stare at him. My pain and depression? Long gone! It's amazing what fear can do. That did it! The bear continued on for seconds and thirds until my basket was empty.

Then he just sat there, next to me, gazing at the creek like he was resting from a full stomach. I prayed! Strangely, something made me relax a little. I, too, gazed out over the water. I cannot explain but, somehow, I knew I was safe. Although, my hands are shaking as I write about it now.

What next came to my mind was that scripture on my bookmark from Isaiah 46:10: "Don't panic. (A great one for when you're sitting next to a bear!) I'm with you. There's no need to fear for I'm your God. I'll give you strength. I'll help you. I'll hold you steady, keep a firm grip on you."

Perhaps God sent the bear to remind me that He Himself is big and powerful, and He is with me.

Little did I know at the time but we were being watched. From a distant, arid hilltop, a small band of the nearby Apache tribe watched the whole scene from their horses. I can hardly imagine what they must have thought!

The bear, bored perhaps, stood up and sloshed back across the creek. He stopped midway and looked back at me with a gnarly growl before disappearing into the thick brush.

I stood up, collected my empty basket and fishing pole, walked a few steps, and then fainted.

When I woke up, I was staring up at Sam (like when I first got here) in front of his house. He looked very wary of the Indian men now lined up on their horses behind me. They had brought me home. Sarah emerged on the porch with the boys who were both fearful of and fascinated with the tribesmen.

As the chief spoke in their language, a younger Apache man beside him translated in fairly good English. I noticed that he wore a calvary-style, double-breasted shirt over blue military-issued pants with gold stripes on the sides.

"Chief Song Owl wants to bestow his friendship to you. He found your wife at the river. She was visited by Bear Spirit. He has ordained her a friend of our people. We will call her Sits With Bear."

I sat up in awe. I have an Indian name? But it was only a hungry bear who found my fish. Wasn't it? And did he say wife?

"She is not my wife," Sam corrected them and indicated Sarah. "She is."

The younger Apache man translated this to Chief Song Owl, who shook his head adamantly and insisted what the young Indian translated as, "You have two wives."

Sarah and Sam looked at each other as the Apache men turned their horses to take their departure.

But Sam raised an arm and called out to them to wait. He hurried to the side of the house and into their cellar the size of a bomb shelter. Gunnar tailed him. They emerged with four big sides of salted beef to give to the Apache men who accepted them.

When the tribesmen rode off, we all sat on the porch so I could explain the whole thing. I was afraid of being chastised for losing a basket full of fish that would have been our dinner; instead, I received hugs and smiles for my safe return. Paul couldn't stop calling me, "Sits With Bear"! Gunnar just eyed me silently.

Friday, October 19, 1877

Sam opened up to me today. I brought lunch out to him and the boys this afternoon. Sarah had gone to call on the Townsends (our next door neighbors five miles away) to get some fabric for a new dress. Anyway, I just can't get over it. He actually *talked* to me.

When I reached them, Sam was resting by some sagebrush drinking the last of his canteen for which I brought a jug full. It was an unusually warm day. As I laid out warm bread and roasted chicken, he started talking.

"So, what do you think he meant?"

"Who?" I asked.

"That chief. Him sayin' I have two wives."

Now, why was he asking me this? Didn't he assume, as had I, that perhaps Chief Song Owl thought this white man just had two wives? Why was he bringing this up? It was not like him to confront issues with me. I mean, Sam is a man of few words. He just says what is necessary to get the daily chores done. This was really out of character for him to actually discuss this.

"Are you gonna answer me?" He broke my pensive silence. I'm sure I showed shock.

"Ah, well…well! I suppose he must have thought, seeing two women, that there were just two wives in this household. Maybe they do have more than one wife," I reasoned.

"You don't think he may have had any other insight?" Sam questioned.

What was he getting at? I was dying to know! And afraid to ask! But all I could do was shrug my shoulders, at a total loss for words. But Sam was not! He went on.

"I've been thinking about how you came to be here: how it is you just showed up one day on my ranch. And maybe it doesn't really matter how you got here. But since you've been with us, it's become clear to me that you now make up part of the family. You've helped the ranch grow and helped get us out of the difficult time we were stuck in for so long. Before you came, I was thinkin' we might have to move. And the Lord only knows where. Now I'm at the point where I can begin thinkin' again about hiring a vaquero or two. Give my boys other options, if they want."

He was mostly speaking of Gunnar, I was sure. Paul might very well follow in his footsteps and inherit the ranch. He admired his pa so and is an especially bright kid.

"You're awfully quiet," Sam pointed out.

"I'm just thinking," I explained. "I don't know where I fit in with your family. I guess I'm like a hired hand."

Sam laughed. "You're more than a hired hand."

Maybe like Alice on *The Brady Bunch*, she was the maid but treated like family. I didn't say that though.

Then he grew serious. "You're much more than that. But I just don't know what exactly."

And then he did something I've been saving for the end! He put his hand on mine and gave it a squeeze.

The boys rode up so he let go. They had the herd clear down by the creek where they left them so they could get lunch. My heart was pounding; my head was spinning. What now?

11

Caught

Saturday, November 3, 1877

We had another town dance in the millhouse tonight. I keep surveying the townsfolk for a potential "someone for me." But it's always the same problem—the available men in Barlow are either too young or too old. Blast!

However, I got to dance with Sam tonight! Yes, that's right! After a quadrille with Sarah, she decided to sit the next one out. A waltz began. With Sarah's approval, Sam offered his hand to me. He led me by the hand, putting his other around my back. As the music started, we began to dance.

And do you know? He looked me in the eye the entire time. I was fixated on him, and the whole room disappeared. For this lovely song, we moved gracefully. For this brief moment in time, it was just him and me, embraced. I'll never forget it, not in all the days of my life.

....

Tuesday, November 6, 1877

Something frightening and terrible has happened today!

We went to town. While Sam and the boys were at Smithy John's (to have nails made to complete the fence round the barn), Sarah and I went to the mercantile for sugar for which we brought a basket of eggs to pay with. If one is low on cash, Mr. Kane will accept things he can sell, like eggs. While Mr. Kane measured out a pound of sugar for us, guess who walked into the shop? Mr. Jethro Mason!

He wanted to speak to Sarah alone but she would not have it. He would have to accept my presence with her. I could not believe what he said.

"Miss Sarah, I only want to express my deepest apologies for the upset I have caused your family, both now and thence. I can never rid myself of the horrible guilt I have carried with me all these years. I only mean to repay you what your father lost along with all interest earned. Please accept my apologies and my irrefragable offer."

He handed Sarah a Barlow Bank cheque for A QUARTER OF A MILLION DOLLARS written out to her from Jethro himself!

And Sarah handed it right back! I could not believe her!

"Consider what, sir?" she retaliated. "Though you make good your debt, you can never repay me for what you have done to my family. To my father's good name. To his life! You destroyed everything he ever worked for. I watched him suffer and deteriorate till his final breath—and it was all due to *you!*"

She composed herself before continuing. "My heart may forgive you, Mr. Mason, out of my Christian duty, but I will never forget!"

"Sarah, please, I beg of you. Give me time to make good between us again."

"There was never anything between us, sir, good or otherwise. Do never speak to me again!"

He tried to stop her from leaving, taking hold of her arm. It was scandalous!

"Forgive me for saying so, ma'am," Jethro went on, "but your beauty has always remained etched in my mind and is branded on my heart for all time. Please, Sarah. I could give you so much more, if only you would consider—"

"I am sure I know nothing of such ugly things you could suggest, sir."

At this point, they both seemed to have forgotten little ol' me standing there gaped.

Sarah whipped her arm out of Jethro's relentless grip and nearly knocked him in the face. I've never seen this side of her before. She was outraged!

"And should you ever attempt to disgrace my family again, sir, I will see to it personally that you are brought to death, if by my own hand!"

You go, girl! And you know what Jethro said?

"Such passion, woman. I never knew you had it in you."

What a smart— (you know what)!

Sarah bid him good afternoon and stormed out the door with a stupefied me in tow. The cheque had fallen to the floor, and I tried not to step on it on my way out. Jethro picked it up and unavailingly watched us leave. Whew! Wee!

Thursday, November 8, 1877

Okay, I need to know what this is all about and somebody better tell me! I've been trying to get hints from Sarah or Sam about what her misfortunate encounter with Mr. Mason was all about and why they detest this man so much. I don't even think Sarah told Sam about our run in with him, nor about the cheque. Sam acts no different, so I'm guessing she has not.

I wonder if Sam would have wanted her to take the money at least? Several times I near told him, as it's stayed on my mind, but Sarah insisted I not tell him or the boys. This is really hard! I can't believe she didn't take the money!

I really need a lock on this book.

12

A Refuge

Monday, November 12, 1877

Oh, dear. What have I done? This morning I awoke especially early and I don't know why. Maybe because it was my birthday, though I've told no one. Maybe because it was ice cold in my room. It must have been four in the morning, but I could not sleep another hour; it was too cold to stay in bed.

So I got dressed and briskly washed my face with the freezing basin water on the front porch. That woke me up! Then I headed out to begin my chores. There was a thick fog resting on the land; I could not see two feet in front of me. So blinding the fog, the barn seemed to materialize out of nothing before my face.

In the barn, Clover filled one pale. I stood and accidentally knocked over a hoe leaning against Sam's work table which, in turn, knocked a hammer off the workbench that fell on my hand still holding the pale.

My hands were already freezing and the heavy metal hammer crushed my knuckles. I was in so much pain! I screamed and cried. Sam came rushing in, already en route.

He took my sore hand in his and rubbed it as the tears streamed down my face. This just made me cry harder. It was like the crack that broke the dam. All my efforts to contain my emotions of late just broke, and they gushed out again. He tried to console me, futilely wiping the tears away until I finally calmed down.

We looked at each other for a long moment, it felt like. He would not let go of my hand. The silvery mist about us made it seem ever more like we were suspended in a dream.

Then we heard, "Pa!"

Gunnar, in the door way, stared at us in disbelief. Sam stepped away from me. Before he could say a word, Gunnar darted for the house. Sam ran after him. I about collapsed.

When I finally made it back to the house, I found Sarah sitting in the Windsor chair by the hearth with her head in her hands.

I left to collect the eggs, completely beside myself as to what to do next. But strangely nothing was ever said. The day continued with our routines, but Sarah remained silent all day. Could I blame her? I am sick with grief and guilt.

It's now eight o'clock at night. I came straight in here after supper dishes were cleaned. The tension has been so thick all day. It is all I can do to keep from running out of the house. But I know what I must do. I must leave. For good.

I'll be destruction to this family if I stay any longer, to this good family. I can't bear it anymore. I must go. Along with my Bible, I will take you with me, diary. You are all I have.

Wednesday, November 14, 1877

I left two nights ago while everyone slept. I was so careful leaving, trying to quietly open the front door that always creaks loudly. I took with me a bundle (wrapped in a shawl that Sarah had taught me to make). Inside were my nightgown and underthings, my toothbrush, a tin of tooth powder, hairbrush, my ink pen and ink well, my Bible, and you, diary. But I was quite cold now, unable to wear the shawl. My bonnet held in some heat on my head.

It was pitch-dark outside. I felt my way to the barn to say good-bye to Feliz. She scampered to the stall door when she heard my voice and greeted me with her youthful baa. It took me longer than I wanted to give her kisses and a big hug. I didn't want to leave her and couldn't help but cry as I left.

After an hour of walking, praying that I was headed toward town, I came to my senses and grew scared. What was I doing?

Frightening sounds beset me of moving brush and heavy breathing. I looked behind me and caught the glint of several pairs of eyes. Coyotes? Wolves? I did not know which. But it was a pack of something, and they were following me!

Frantic, I quickened my pace, crying out, "Oh, God, please help me! Save me, God! Please save me, Lord! Please, Jesus, save me!"

I kept screaming in prayer and ran until I could run no more. Under normal circumstances, I would have collapsed from exhaustion long before, but my overwhelming fear and adrenaline kept me going.

It grew silent. Warily, I slowed down and looked behind me. They were gone, whatever they were. No more eyes.

"Praise you, Lord Jesus! Thank you, Lord Jesus! Oh, thank you! Thank you for saving me!" I cried over and again.

I recalled a scripture Sarah read to us one night. (I miss terribly already.)

> "I sought the Lord, and He heard me, and delivered me from all my fears." (Ps. 34:4, KJV)

Ahead the horizon was aglow from the town—the lights of Jethro Mason's hotel in full swing, to be exact. I didn't care. I followed it as though it were a beacon in the night.

And so, now, I sit here in a room of my own in the Pristine Hotel of Barlow. This can't be happening.

Friday, November 16, 1877

I am uncomfortable, scared, and know not what to do.

> For the Spirit that God has given us does not make us timid; instead, His Spirit fills us with power, love, and self-control. (2 Tim. 1:7, GNT)

Oh, self-control. What's that?

Where am I writing this? Inside the noisy saloon of Jethro Mason's hotel. I am hiding behind the bar, sitting on a barrel. No one is paying me any mind. There is too much going on in this fully lit room (in more ways than one). There is the jarring tones of Elmer banging away on the piano forte, the ruckus of men playing cards and harassing the saloon girls who wait on them, drinks spilling and clanging over shouts and cheers, and the thumping and screeching of chairs as drunken men get up or down.

What? Am I hallucinating? I have had a few shots of absinthe that Marcelle, the head mistress here, keeps giving me to "ease my nerves." The room is spinning. Yet I think I see, through the crowd and thick pipe smoke, a man sitting calmly at a game table. He has a very familiar face with long brown hair, a mustache and beard, and those beautiful eyes that touch your soul. But He dons common clothes and a wide-brimmed hat. I almost did not recognize Him—the Lord. He is looking at me and, with His eyes, He is saying something I recognize as Scripture but I don't know it.

"Let your conversation be without covetousness, and be content with such things as ye have: for He hath said, I will never leave thee, nor forsake thee. So that we may boldly say, 'The Lord is my helper, and I will not fear what man shall do unto me.'"

He's gone. Someone else is sitting where he sat. I'm being called by Marcelle. A burly man is coming my way. He's gross. I have to go.

November 17, 1877, 2:20 a.m.

I'm alone now. I'm shaking yet exhausted. I couldn't do it with this man. He tried to make me. I fought him with all my might. I hit and kicked, but he was stronger. However, I managed to pull my feet up and kick him off me. He flew across the room and shattered a standing mirror. Half-dressed, I ran out of the room, down the stairs, through the saloon, and out into the cold air I gulped in.

I was soon caught by some men from the saloon. They put me in Constable Dunn's office until Jethro came to retrieve me. He was furious. Now I'm back in my room at the hotel. Alone, thankfully. But he locked me in here. I'm so tired but I need to read something to calm down enough to sleep. Is it possible to be both anxious and exhausted at the same time? I guess so.

Oh, I like this one from Psalm 62:8 (GNT): "Trust in God at all times, my people. Tell Him all your troubles, for He is our refuge."

Lord Jesus, I just miss the Egans. I miss Sam. I miss my baby, Feliz. All this I lay at Your feet. I just release it all to You, Lord. It's all in Your care. I'm feeling better. I think I can go to sleep now.

Jethro just came in! Now I'm stressed out again. HANG HIM! I'm shaking so hard, I can hardly write. He flew in the room and grabbed me by the neck, almost choking me to death.

He yelled, "You're going to ruin my business! I can't have you in the saloon behaving so contemptibly. Do you hear?"

I cried, "I have to go back. I made a mistake coming here. I have to go back."

He loosened his grip on me, but his eyes still hinted malice. "You want to return to the Egans? Do you wish to destroy that family?"

I would never do that! How dare he! But was he right? Would what happened in the barn inevitably happen again at some point, had I stayed? Did I have so strong an attraction to Sam, that it could drive me beyond all reason and self-control? And did Sam me?

Yes, I must stay away from Sam, at all cost, even my own life. And then! You won't believe what Jethro next said!

"I'm going to do what's best for you. I'm going to marry you and take you far away from here."

Then he stormed out and locked me in again.

I'm horrified. I can't leave Barlow! Being in town keeps me, if only, on the edge of Sam's life. I can't lose the hope of chance seeing him when he comes to town.

Lord, I need you. Please, what have I done?

> They go to Egypt for help without asking for My advice. They want Egypt to protect them, so they put their trust in Egypt's king. (Isa. 30:2, GNT)

That's what I've done, Lord, isn't it? I've put my trust in "King" Mason. The thought never even entered my mind to ask You for Your advice before I ran off to what I thought was the perfect solution to all my problems. Instead, I panicked. Now, I don't know what to do.

I want to die. Please, Lord, just let me die.

> "The Sovereign Lord, the Holy One of Israel, says to the people, 'Come back and quietly trust in Me. Then you will be strong and secure.' But you refuse to do it. Instead, you plan to escape from your enemies by riding fast horses. And you are right—escape is what you will have to do! You think your horses are fast enough, but those who pursue you will be faster! And yet the Lord is waiting to be merciful to you. He is ready to take pity on you because He always does what is right. Happy are those who put their trust in the Lord." (Isa. 30:15–18, GNT)

Sunday, November 18, 1877
I just saw Sam! This is horrible.

For starts, Jethro would not let me go to church. He has me locked in my room except at night when they send me down to work in the saloon. All night I'm under constant surveillance by that nazi, Marcelle. I can't leave this hotel. It's the "Hotel California!" Aggh!

Then at midday today, I saw out my window–Sam! He must have come here after church. I saw him go into the hotel and, moments later, come back out. I banged on my window in the top corner of the building, but he did not hear me nor turn around. He kept going down the bustling street. My guess is he stopped in to see if I was here and whomever he talked to must have told him they've never seen me or don't know who I am.

Tuesday, November 20, 1877

I just dreamt for the first time since I've been away from the Egans about living with them. It was so haunting. I felt like I was really there again.

All I remember is that it was mostly about Paul. He was sitting at the table under the glow of an oil lamp in the dark. I must have been sitting across from him as I did many times, teaching him how to read, mostly from the Bible. He was reading it now. But he looked at me, rather than the book, as he recited Proverbs 3:25–26. (KJV):

"Be not afraid of sudden fear, neither of the desolation of the wicked, when it cometh. For the LORD shall be thy confidence, and shall keep thy foot from being taken."

He stared at me with these powerful, serene eyes—the eyes of Lord Jesus. It woke me abruptly.

Thursday, November 22, 1877

This evening, Jethro and I supped alone in the dining room in back of the hotel. We ate silently. You could hear the fire in the hearth crackle and spit loudly. I could make out Jethro's face, in its fiery glow, intent on his plate. With courage, I mustered up conversation.

"I'm all right with going to Ridge City with you," I announced.

Still, I couldn't bring myself to say the "marrying you" part just yet. I was hoping he would know what I meant without having to add that. Jethro dropped his knife and fork on his plate and folded his hands, taking me in with ice cold eyes. Did he believe me?

"Well," he said, "what brings this sudden change of heart?"

I dropped my head. It was difficult to know what to say next, to keep my voice from quivering and to keep from crying.

"I know it's for the best. I need to be far away from the Egans. I never should have been with them in the first place. It was wrong from the start. And I believe it's what the Lord wants."

I finally looked at him again. His eyes were still harsh and it put a chill down my spine. Then I realized that must not have been the answer he was hoping for. I suspect he wanted to hear that I wanted to go away with him, that I might love him. Oops.

But before I could add more, Jethro stood and took his leave.

13

The Letter to Sarah

Monday, November 26, 1877

I know it's been some days but I've been kept very busy. Something happened tonight that has made me most afraid. With Jethro planning to marry me and take me to Ridge City Monday of next week, I've already begun to receive wifely duties at the hotel, including washing Jethro's clothes (of which he has a lot). This man has more underwear than any man I've ever known. Cotton long johns is what they wear. Sam only has two pair. Jethro must have twenty!

Anyway, I was folding and putting away his undergarments when I spotted an envelope under a pair tucked in back of his top bureau drawer. I pulled it out. It was a letter to Sarah Egan from him that apparently was returned to him unopened. I recognized it immediately as the letter Sarah received way back from the pony express kid. I never got to see it. So it *was* from Jethro! No wonder Sam was so indignant.

Now here it was in my hand. Whatever possessed me (I suppose curiosity that bordered desperation to find out more), I opened it. That was all it took to make me risk everything to read it. As I did, my eyes grew wide.

Then the door to Jethro's bedchamber flew open behind me. I froze. Heavy footsteps creaked on the floorboards towards me as a deep voice cleared its throat. I knew it was Jethro without turning around. He ripped the letter out of my grasp and, without further ado, began to read it aloud.

August 22, 1877

My dearest Sarah,

You may not wish to hear from me, and I apologize on my intrusion if it causes you great distress. But I have unfinished business I must conclude.

As you know, the last of my dealings with your father involved a large investment of his fortune, along with the financial contribution of the North Bank of Boston, placed into a transport company that was done with great faith in me. It is true that I never owned such a corporation, as I had led them to believe that could reap great profits at wartime: shipping men and artillery to battle fronts. I will never be able to tell you why I led them astray as I am sworn to secrecy for the rest of my life.

But what your father and the founders of North Bank did not come to know was that I had invested all of their funds into oil and iron companies. Subsequently, their money quadrupled in value over the course of the war. I am now in position to return all moneys invested to their rightful owners.

It bereaves me to learn that your late father succumbed to illness and an untimely death. It shall never fully console me to know that I can never repay him directly. But if I may return to you and your family his full and complete investment with all interest earned, it would give me the greatest satisfaction.

I long to tell you personally how deeply sorry I am for my deception and all the pain I have caused your family to suffer. I wish I could give you much more than this monetary compensation, but I know full well that I shall have to remain satisfied to this end alone.

Please find enclosed a cheque for the amount of your dear father's investment and four times its earnings.

I bid you a good life and my sincerest apologies once more. I will never forget you, my dearest Sarah. Forgive my forwardness but, forever more, you will remain branded on my heart.

I remain yours
to the last,
Mr. Jethro Mason

I'm still holding the letter and that is it, word for word! He gave it back to me, saying, "Well, you wished to know." Then he told me everything.

His story aligns with Sarah's. He said he met Sarah before she married Sam when she went by her maiden name:

Gunnarsson. Sarah's father, a highly respected manager of the North Bank of Boston, took a great liking to Jethro Mason, then a young businessman who came to offer him a financial opportunity.

Mr. Gunnarsson even thought as far as considering this debonair young gentleman as a potential husband for his eldest daughter, Sarah, then seventeen. But she already fancied another who had recently enlisted in the Union Army. Guess who?

Sam Egan came from a poor family "and was not her father's choice for a suitor" (as Jethro put it). But Sarah's father encouraged a match with Mr. Mason who, though able to charm Sarah, could not manage to surpass the "foolish affections that blinded her in her youth" (J's words).

Jethro also told me that he has never since loved another woman as he did Sarah, unrequited though it remained.

Nonetheless, he did persuade Mr. Gunnarsson (as well as the bank institution) to invest a great amount of their fortunes into this presumed transport company (that they later were to learn did not exist). Jethro then left on urgency but promised to return, and Sarah's father assured him that she would be waiting.

Five years passed and the war ended before Jethro Mason could return with the Gunnarsson's money, now a much greater fortune. But it was already too late. Sarah had gone out west somewhere, married and with her first child. In complete despair, having suffered so much loss including that of his own long-established reputation, Mr. Gunnarsson had since fallen ill and perished. Hmph. But had Jethro the decency to return his money to the widowed Mrs. Gunnarsson? No!

But it's not over! I was furious at Jethro and yelled at him. How could he steal from the woman he claimed to love and hurt her family like that? His lame answer was he was not at liberty to explain. He further argued that, all those years, he has been trying to return to Sarah what was owed her family. That's why he came to Barlow and sent the letter and cheque by express only to have it returned unopened, uninvited.

I acknowledge that his intentions were good but I am not satisfied with what I know. There is more to this and I intend to find it out. And hopefully before I get to Ridge City with this beastly, deceitful man! Maybe Jethro Mason isn't even his real name! My ink is lo—

....

Tuesday, November 27, 1877

Got more ink today. I dreamt about Sam and Jethro last night. We were back at Paramount Ranch in my time again. It started the same way. I see them arrive on the train platform. They walk down the dirt street toward me. And still they did not know me, not even Sam. Makes me want to hum the old song, "You Don't Know Me." LOL! Whoa, did I write that?

I remember I wrote that on a note once, without thinking, for Ms. Schumacher.

She wrinkled her nose at me and retorted, "L-O-L is not a word." I didn't dare try to explain

Okay, the dream. This one was sweet. Oh, Sam. I really felt this time a sense of what is unspoken between us. At first, we all just spoke in generalities, introductions out of the way. Sam looked like his mind was elsewhere the whole time.

Then Jethro, who kept looking at me, said, "You looked troubled."

I was. I was fixed on Sam, who was so lost in thought, staring at the fire we sat around in the center of the desolate town at night.

The silence grew uncomfortable, so I broke it. "Let's play a game. I Spy. I'll start first. I spy…a fire."

Jethro smirked. Sam finally looked my way.

"I spy," Jethro carried on, staring me full in the eyes. "I spy four Yankees."

I woke right up. Weird!

14

I Spy

Wednesday, November 28, 1877

Early this morning, Jethro and I left Barlow by stagecoach for Ridge City about fifty miles away, which might as well be a thousand. It's a twelve-hour stage ride with four stops.

It was so hard to leave. I could not tear my eyes away from out the back window, watching Barlow slowly diminish from sight for the last time. I saw the school in the distance with the church beyond it, Mr. Kane's mercantile, Constable's Dunn's jail next to Smithy John's, and the millhouse where my dream briefly came true at the town dance. Oh, my! The many times I had come to Barlow with the Egans to buy goods. Teaching with ol' Ms. Schumacher. The Sunday picnics.

It felt like it was years I had spent here with the Egans. For a while, I was part of their family, a part of the life of the only man who had ever touched my soul. I'll never forget them. Never. My tears are staining my ink. I must stop.

Thursday, November 29, 1877

I'm in the newly built Pristine Hotel of Ridge City, alone in my own luxurious quarters overlooking the main street of this bigger, busier town. I'm so depressed. I will read my Bible.

> God is the One who has prepared us for this change, and He gave us His Spirit as the guarantee of all that He has in store for us. (2 Cor. 5:5, GNT)

Am I prepared for this change? I still want to die, Lord.

Friday, November 30, 1877

I can't bear it anymore. I must go back to them. I must go back to the Egans. I cannot stop thinking about Sam. I don't know why or how, but somehow, some way, I really belong with him. I know I do. It was like Chief Song Owl said; Sam has two wives. I know it. Eventually, it would have, and could, become that way if it were God's will.

Why else was I there? How else could I have gone back in time to them if not by God's will? Somehow I must go back! WE MUST GO BACK, DIARY! I'm so afraid something terrible will become of me if I stay with Jethro any longer. Oh Lord, I'm so afraid!

Remember that I have commanded you to be
determined and confident! Do not be afraid or
discouraged, for I, the Lord your God, am with you
wherever you go. (Josh. 1:9, GNT)

Saturday, December 1, 1877

Oh my goodness! I can scarcely get my breath. Jethro is not
about, and I know not where. So I took the chance tonight
to go into his chamber in search of money. I have this one
chance to grab some and leave, to take the next stage back to
Barlow. It may be my only chance until I know not when. I
have to take it.

I also hoped to find the cheque written to Sarah but could
not find it, nor were there any bill notes to be found. Blast!

So I neatened his underwear and shut the bureau drawer
swiftly because Brunella walked in and eyed me suspiciously
as I leaned against Jethro's bureau. Brunella is the headmistress
of Ridge City's Pristine Hotel Saloon. She is a stocky Italian
woman with a mop of black curls and a face that would be
cute if it were not scrunched up in anger, half the time, like
Edward G. Robinson. She is the boss of everybody here. Tall
and sturdy, she could be a linebacker. Ugh. Why does Jethro
always hire such abominable women for headmistress?

Now, get this. She drags me down to the bar saying I was
supposed to be working. Jethro's orders. I said she must be
sorely mistaken; I am Mrs. Mason. She said these instructions
came from Jethro himself. I asked where he was because he'd

been gone since morning. She said she didn't know. Yvette (another saloon girl from France) squinted at me like she knew something but I was unable to talk to her.

Goodness, I must go to sleep. I'm exhausted. I did my best to act nauseous every time some grubby man tried to pick me up for "business." I feigned vomiting on their shoes so they would pass me by. But I can't do this forever. If Brunella figures out why I'm not getting any customers, she's gonna whip me for sure!

Sunday, December 2, 1877

I got up at the crack of dawn to go through Jethro's bureau again—nothing there but too much underwear.

But under a window next to his bed sits a big trunk. It was locked but I had to get into it! I took a bobby pin from my hair and jiggled it inside the lock. It would not budge. I got so frustrated that I kicked it several times. Then I lifted one end of the heavy thing and pushed it over. It crashed onto the floor! I froze. But no one stirred as far as I could hear, probably because they were all passed out from late night and liquor. I picked the big trunk back upright and was relieved (and terrified) to see that the lock had broken!

How would I explain that? Well, I couldn't worry about that now. I had only a moment to go through its contents lest anyone intruded and discovered what I was about.

What I found inside was astonishing.

First, I found a note, a written order, made out to Jethro Mason in 1861 to inaugurate him as an official spy for the United States of America "to seek out threats to our nation and to protect its assets, monetary or otherwise." It was even signed by President Abraham Lincoln! This was not a copy; it was the real thing. I could not believe it.

Then it hit me. My dream! The last one I had about Sam, Jethro, and myself at Paramount Ranch. What did Jethro say to me?

"I spy four Yankees."

Or did he mean, "I spy *for* Yankees"?

Maybe that was the dream's meaning. Could Jethro Mason have been a spy for the North during the Civil War? Was this Jethro's secret reason for why he had to leave the Gunnarsson's in a hurry years ago? Was he taking their money, not to steal it, but to protect it from possible Confederate raids? He had said he was sworn to secrecy for life.

But before I even allowed my respect for him to begin to grow, I had to remind myself that he did profiteer the Gunnarssons's savings. He built his hotel business with it and made a fortune off of them (and the North Bank of Boston), leaving them penniless.

Plus, he waited all these years to return it to Sarah. Or did it just take him this long to find her again? After all, she had moved out west. And her father had died by then. Still. He was still a conniving thief out for his own wants and not to be trusted.

There was more! The trunk also held wanted posts with Jethro's face on it issued by the US government. He was to be arrested for fraud, extortion, and embezzlement. Well, that's more like it.

"Wanted: Dead or Alive." Whoa. One reward was one hundred thousand dollars! Oh, I wish he was here. I'd knock him out with a bottle of whiskey and drag him in by his beard for that amount! Being that a loaf of bread costs ten cents, a hundred thousand dollars here is like two million dollars in my time!

Then, as if that weren't enough, underneath the wanted posts, was our marriage certificate I had never got to see.

Oh, no, he didn't. OH, YES, HE DID!

So this was why he wouldn't let me sign it but said it was all taken care of. This wedding certificate, dated the day we got legally married, after we arrived in Ridge City, married Jethro and Sarah Mason! Now, I don't recall a time when Jethro said that I'd be going by the name "Sarah." This could only mean one thing. But what? If I have to spend Christmas with this man, I'm going to be very upset!

And I couldn't find what I really hoped to—the cheque Jethro wrote to Sarah. I wanted so badly to get it back to her.

I found a leather billfold, but all it contained were two tickets for passage to Paris, France from New York—one way. Strange. I could not put those back for fear I may not get to rummage through his trunk again. So I took the tickets, shut the trunk, and dashed out.

15

Home at Last

Tuesday, December 4, 1877

I'm writing this on the stage to Barlow, which is difficult because it's so bumpy. I'm going home! I finally got to talk to Yvette before I left. She told me a mouthful. I learned how she came to be working in the Pristine Hotel Saloon and that her son, Aubrey, was fathered by a customer she had eight years ago.

Aubrey always picked on me because of my name. He said I have a boy's name, which he always stoutly pronounces "Re-*ne*!" So I told him, "Well, where I come from, your name is a girl's name. Aubrey! Thus, he always scoffed at me whenever he saw me. Little brat. No, he's a good kid. Sometimes I'd play games with him—marbles, jacks, or pick-up sticks.

Anyway, Yvette told me she met Jethro Mason, ten years ago, in her home village of Aubeterre, a distance southeast of

Paris. He brought her to America promising her a good life and marriage. They journeyed to Ridge City where he opened his Pristine Hotel. Then he put her in the saloon to work. I know! Pig. Penniless, she had no other option.

A year later, she became pregnant by who knows whom. And when Aubrey was born, it became impossible for her to save money having to feed and care for both she and her son. She has been trying to save, little by little, all these years in hopes to one day return to her village and her family. I nearly cried when I heard this.

"So," she told me, "it appears that Jethro has done the same damage to you: to promise marriage and then abandon you at the saloon."

I was dumped! By a man I found nothing more than repulsive. I felt rejected! How could he do that to me? To her? We've been dumped by the scum of the earth!

But then I remembered what I had hidden in my diary upstairs. I went to get it and gave it to Yvette immediately— the two one-way tickets to Paris! Tears filled her eyes. She could not believe it. We hugged as she cried and cried, elated.

I gave her the money I saved from meager tips I earned serving drinks and, with hers, it was enough to get her and her son on a train to New York with some to spare for food. I gave her my wedding ring for good measure. That should be worth a good twenty dollars. They are leaving tomorrow! Hurrah! Praise God.

When she rushed off to tell Aubrey, for a mere instant I thought I saw a man looking at me from outside a saloon window. It looked like the Lord. His stare hit me like lightning and a thought struck me.

Jethro Mason must have disappeared to Barlow to take away Sarah! He must be planning to kidnap, or coerce, her to go as his legal wife to Paris! That must be his twisted plan. But how could he take her with Sam around? Or did he have a plan for that too? He must!

So I grabbed my coat, Bible, diary, and bonnet. I flew down the two staircases to the hotel lobby and out the door. Brunella chased me all the way down, yelling at the top of her lungs. Someone had told her about my pretend-to-barf strategy to avoid customers, and she was beet red with anger. It was probably that windbag, Eloise. She hated me, too. Who cares! I was out of here!

I ran with all my might to the stage depot. The next stage to Barlow was about to leave! It was six o'clock this morning. Then I realized I had no money for passage. I had given it all to Yvette. The ticket manager was not about to let me get on.

"I'm Mrs. Jethro Mason!" I exclaimed. But I had not my gold ring to show him. He just raised his eyebrows, so I rephrased. "I mean, I work for Mr. Mason in the saloon."

He crossed his arms and nodded with better acceptance of my second explanation.

"As a matter of fact, you can credit my fare to the saloon. Ask for Brunella."

He agreed! (And chuckled with a twinkle in his eye. Hmm!) Well, must make note never to return to Ridge City lest I run into Brunella again. I feel bad about my deceitfulness. I know it was wrong. Forgive me, Lord! But this was an emergency! I didn't know what else to do!

....

4:15 p.m.

I just arrived in Barlow and am sitting in C. Dunn's office. When I got off the coach, I was alarmed to see a unit of US Army officers scouting the main street, talking to folks, inquiring about something.

Then I heard, "There she is! Get her!"

I turned to see a ruffled man come after me with a wanted post in his hand. Behind him trailed Constable Dunn and the four federal officers. What did I do now?

"This is her. This here is Jethro Mason's wife, officers," Constable presented me as. Eck!

The rowdy man beside the constable grabbed hold of me, and I got a good look at the wanted post.

> WANTED: Alive
> MRS. JETHRO MASON
> REWARD: $40

Forty dollars! I'm insulted. And sketched on it was the most hideous portrait of me I'd ever seen! Definitely not the one Jethro drew in the schoolhouse. I looked like the Wicked Witch of the West after she got smashed by Dorothy's house.

Immediately, the man started asking the Constable for his *re*ward, and the officers started questioning me about Jethro's whereabouts. But my mind was on just one thing:

"WHO DREW THIS PORTRAIT? And how many of them are posted around town?" I screamed over their voices.

One strapping officer with a dark horseshoe mustache and long sideburns, apparently the one in charge, asked me pointedly, "Where is your husband, ma'am?"

Dead, I hope.

But I responded, "I cannot say, but I suspect he has gone to the Egan ranch."

I suddenly recalled the danger Sarah, Sam, and the boys must be in. We had to hurry!

Now I'm sitting in C. Dunn's office, waiting impatiently for the horses to be saddled up so we can go. I insisted on going with them. 'Course, their only allowing me to because they most surely will be in want of more information.

They're ready. Gotta go!

10:40 p.m.

Wow, I got to ride with the calvary. I rode with one of the officers. It took an hour to reach the Egan homestead at a gallop. We slowed as we approached the back of our (I mean, their) barn—an endearing sight for my sore eyes.

The closer we got, I began to make out a man and woman near the house. He was attempting to help her mount his horse. The lady was Sarah. The man, as I feared, was Jethro.

"Sarah!" I screamed.

They both looked to us. Immediately, Jethro clutched Sarah round her neck. With his free hand, he drew his pistol and shot one of the officers off his horse, wounding him in his side.

We came to a halt, and Jethro put his pistol to Sarah's head. Oh, yes, he did! The officers and C. Dunn drew their guns.

"Mr. Mason," the officer in charge called. "You are under arrest by the authority of the federal government. Release the woman and lay down your gun at once."

I had to glance at him. Really? Did he really think Jethro Mason would oblige? I grew scared that Jethro would really shoot Sarah. But, at the same time, I could not believe him! The very woman who has burned in his heart for so many years…could he really kill her? As if in response, Jethro cocked the hammer of his shotgun, the barrel pinned to Sarah's temple.

It was growing dark more rapidly now and it felt like forever that we remained in position.

Then we heard a loud gunshot. A bullet ricocheted off the dirt near J.'s horse's hind hoof. Buckshot (the horse) reared up and kicked Jethro in the head (like so many times I wished he would have done in the past).

Everything happened so quickly. Jethro lost control of Sarah who fled to us. He recovered his step and fired into the darkness before I could see at whom he was shooting.

Sarah screamed, "Sam!"

My heart stopped. Then I saw three figures approach from afar and knew at once it was Sam and the boys.

Then the lead Calvary officer shot Jethro square in his chest. Jethro bled from his heart.

The officers dismounted. Sarah grabbed onto me, sobbing. I held her tight, shaking as well.

We stood around the fallen Jethro, watching him die. He was up on his knees, dazed, as his blood flowed like a trickling waterfall onto the ground. He turned his eyes up at Sarah. For the first time I'd ever known him, Jethro Mason looked pathetic. Tears dripped down his cheeks. Then he collapsed in a heap.

Sarah ran to Sam and the boys. Sam was holding his shoulder, wounded. Then I noticed that Gunnar was hurt too. His left arm was wrapped in his blue scarf soaked in blood. He looked in shock.

Constable Dunn yelled, "I'll call on the doc!" and tore off on his horse.

The lead officer searched Jethro's body while the Egans and I sat on the front porch. Paul lit a lantern, which blanketed us with soft light. The chief officer brought forth an envelope, seeped with blood, for Sarah.

"I believe this is for you, Mrs. Egan."

She knew what it was—the cheque for $250,000. At last, she accepted it.

Some time passed before Doctor Schaeffer arrived and tended to Sam and Gunnar. They had both been shot: one bullet went through Sam's shoulder, the other only brushed Gunnar's arm. Sam's condition is serious, but Doc Schaeff cleaned his wound and feels he will be fine.

Sarah ended the day with a scripture.

> For the Lord loveth judgment, and forsaketh not
> His saints; they are preserved for ever: but the seed
> of the wicked shall be cut off. (Ps. 37:28, KJV)

I couldn't help but pray for Jethro tonight. Despite all the suffering he caused for so many in his lifetime, I prayed that he was able to—in his final moments—repent to Jesus and return to Him. I cannot wish eternal hell on even the worst of us.

It's amazing. Here I thought I messed up my life by acting on my own discretion, without consulting God. Still, He took hold of the whole mess I made and resolved everything capitally, even making Sarah at last take the money so sorely overdue her.

> We know that in all things God works for good
> with those who love Him, those whom He has
> called according to His purpose. (Rom. 8:28, GNT)

I've just come in from hugging and kissing little, woolly Feliz in her stall who greeted me with her familiar "maa." She's so cute. She acts like I never left, God bless her.

I must go to bed. I'm falling asleep. I am back in my room. I'm so happy, I'm weeping. We are home, diary. Home at last.

16

Don't Panic

Tuesday, December 4, 2015

Oh, my! Did I write that? What on earth made me write that? That's weird.

This morning at breakfast, I found out more of what had happened to Sam and the boys, and to Sarah, leading up to when I had arrived with the officers and Constable Dunn.

Sam and the boys were out near the creek with the herd when Paul spotted a man standing beyond the cattle. And then another. There were about ten men in all surrounding them. Paul said he saw a gun aimed right at him. But before he could move, his broken saddle slid sideways again and dropped him onto the ground as he heard gun fire. Thank God his saddle was broken!

Then lots of guns fired into the herd. The steer went haywire. Sam dropped to the ground and covered Paul behind a fallen steer, yelling at Gunnar to dismount.

Gunnar (as he says) was already ahead of him. He lept off his horse and hid behind a big rock. Sam fired back at the men, but it was hopeless. The cattle had run away, leaving him and the boys wide open.

Two armed men flanked Sam and Paul, aiming at their faces. Paul said he was sure they were going to die, so he closed his eyes. (He demonstrated this by squishing his eyes shut.) Then he heard "the wind get slit in two" as he put it. Paul opened his eyes to see the two men in front of them fall forward with arrows in their backs.

Up on a plateau hid several of Chief Song Owl's tribesmen. They had come to their rescue!

Still, one man shot again, hitting Gunnar's arm. As the man closed in for another shot, Sam fired at him but missed!

He screamed, "Leave my boy!"

The man went to finish Gunnar anyway but before he could fire, a loud roar startled him from behind. I could not believe what it was! It was a bear charging him! It rose up on its hind legs and towered over the man who dropped his gun and ran for his life. The bear chased him away.

Gunnar said he believed me now about the bear. It must have been my bear friend, I'm sure! I asked him to describe his coat and growl, but Gunnar just wrinkled his nose at me. Everyone laughed.

Then it was Sarah's turn to tell her happenstances. She was alone in the house, washing dishes, when she heard a horse approach. Assuming it was Sam or one of the boys, she looked out the kitchen window and must have gone pale. For the man was not Sam but Jethro Mason.

She grabbed a fire poker from the hearth (which the boys found amusing) to take with her to the front door.

Jethro told her he heard shooting down by the river, and there were bodies everywhere. The constable was there (he lied) and requested that she go identify three bodies as possibly her husband and sons. Jethro said he believed it was bandits that attacked them.

Sarah could not remember what happened next but she knows that she dropped the poker on the porch because it was not in her hand when she stood by Jethro's horse. Then the calvary and the constable showed up with me. I feel faint just writing all this.

Tuesday, December 11, 1877

It's been a week but Jethro's blood still stains the ground outside the house. I can't help but stare at it every time I come out. This morning, I stopped to take a longer look. It bothered me. Jethro was so ruthless going after Sarah. He never let up till it killed him.

I felt that, in a way, I was the same about Sam. I could not stay away from him, or the Egan family, for that matter.

I did everything I could to leave them but I had to come back. Didn't Jethro, too, try to avoid Sarah by marrying me? Oh, I forgot. He had intended to marry her all along. I was just part of his ugly ploy to get Sarah and take her to Paris. Never mind!

But I could bear it no more. I ran. I ran as far as I could until I about collapsed. There was one thing that neither Jethro nor I ever tried to do that mattered most—we never tried to release the objects of our desires. Not realizing that holding on, refusing to let go, would eventually consume us and break down our limited human resistance. It would destroy us. Already it had destroyed Jethro. It's only a matter of time before it would me too, I reckon.

"But I can't fight it alone, Lord!" I heard myself cry out when I could run no more.

The only way for me to release this wrong from my heart was to hand it over to Jesus so I could rely on His strength, which is faultless and unlimited. Who wouldn't want that?

I recited the verse on my ol' bookmark (Isaiah 46:10). "Don't panic. I'm with you. There's no need to fear for I'm your God. I'll give you strength. I'll help you. I'll hold you steady, keep a firm grip on you."

On the horizon, I caught a glimpse of what looked like Jesus standing there. Or was I just imagining Him? But He was gone before I could finish registering what I saw.

Thursday, December 13, 1877

I am up late tonight. I can't sleep, not since that night Jethro was killed. You'd think I'd be sleeping like a baby now, right? The officers said they were actually glad to bring Jethro in dead rather than alive. He had disgraced the US government far too much to be allowed imprisonment. Sheesh!

I'm just so agitated! I'm all distress and I don't know why. I think it's realizing how similar I am to Jethro in my relentless feelings toward Sam. It bothers me to see this in myself. Of course, I would never act upon it. But hadn't I already?

I think about that morning in the barn when we almost… did what? I perish the thought. Or am I being presumptuous to think Sam would do something? Still, should Sam ever do anything inappropriate, I don't know what I'd do. I know I couldn't. Oh, let's be honest! The Lord would have to strike me down with lightning to stop me! Agh!

Can adultery be committed with the mind? Is just thinking about someone who's married a sin? Let's see. Jesus said, "But now I tell you: anyone who looks at a woman and wants to possess her is guilty of committing adultery with her in his heart" (Matt. 5:28, GNT).

I guess so. But He did say, "anyone who looks at a woman," not a man. "L-O-L."

"L-O-L is not a word." That will haunt me forever.

Oh, I have broken this commandment every day that I've been here! I've become enslaved to my own feelings. I know

I really should not stay with him, with them, any longer. But where would I go now?

Friday, December 14, 1877

Today, while we were making bread dough, Sarah said to me, "You've been awfully quiet lately."

"I've just been thinking a lot," I responded. But it was hard to talk really.

"What of?" she asked.

I couldn't answer her. What could I say? That I'm in love with your husband?

"Well," I started, "with your change of fortune, plans to build onto the ranch, and hire on more hands, it doesn't seem practical to have me to take care of anymore."

It was the best way I could put it. I smiled so as not to appear belligerent.

Sarah pulled her fingers out of the dough and rubbed off sticky bits onto her apron. Then she placed her hands on my shoulders with such a look in her eyes. I wanted to cry.

"My dear," she said, "you are family. You're like a sister to me and an aunt to the boys."

Darn it. I cried. Dang glands!

"Sam thinks of you…" she hesitated. I know she knew. "As family, too. We love having you with us. Please don't think that we should ever want you to leave. Who knows? Perhaps Sam will hire a man one day you might take as your husband?"

It was all I could do to keep from running out of the house. Then, strangely, I got a funny thought and chuckled. Sarah giggled in innocence and hugged me.

I was thinking. Suppose I should go with Sam when he hires men so I could pick out the ones I liked! Maybe I could make him jealous by picking out only the really handsome ones. Heh-heh. Okay, stop!

Oh! I must get out of here! But I don't want to! Agh! Good night.

Monday, December 17, 1877

Sam went ahead without me today and hired one Mexican and two white vaqueros: one's badly bucktoothed; one has an Adam's apple the size of an apricot; and the other is so bowlegged, you could roll a giant tumbleweed through his legs. Sam hired them on purpose. I know it!

It is amusing and apparent that Sam is uncomfortable with being a boss. He's so used to doing all the work himself; he is shy when instructing the men. They are nice fellas, I have to say. Don't know where he found them though.

Wednesday, December 19, 1877

I've been getting up earlier than usual. Although, I've been deprived of sleep lately, trying to make up my mind to leave. And when. And how. It wakes me up before dawn. So I've been able to be done in the barn before Sam comes in to tack up Grant.

This morning, however, he caught up to my schedule and addressed me about it. It was still dark outside, and I was filling up the second bucket with Clover.

"You're in here early," he greeted.

"I'm an early bird," I chirped.

"Yeah, quite often." He moved in closer. He hunched down next to me sitting on the stubby milk stool.

"You know," he began, "you're not going have to work so hard soon. We're going to be hiring more hands to do most of the chores."

"I know," I said.

"But don't think it will be any different, how you are to us. You very well know that you are welcome to stay on as long as you like. Our home is your home. You're family. I thought you knew that by now."

I stopped milking and turned around to be polite, fighting back tears.

"Thanks," was all I could utter.

9:20 p.m.

Still up. Listening to the crickets just outside my window—a welcomed sound that usually lulls me to sleep like a lullaby—but not tonight. Though I feel the warm glow of my oil lamp paint my face with light, I am lost in the darkness outside.

I'm stuck on a verse I just read in my Bible and can't stop chewing on the back of my metal ink pen. Have you read it? (I'm asking my diary!) In Matthew 10:38 (GNT) Jesus says, "Whoever does not take up his cross and follow in My steps is not fit to be My disciple."

Even before that, in Matthew 10:37, Jesus states, "Whoever loves his father or mother more than Me is not fit to be My disciple; whoever loves his son or daughter more than Me is not fit to be My disciple."

I heard these passages explained this way before: If we love God over and above all else, then we are able to love and serve our families even more so because we are then able to love them with God's unconditional love. This means we will have more patience, compassion, care, grace, forgiveness, and mercy toward the ones we love dearly (and toward others, for that matter).

I thought about that dream I had months ago about Jesus calling me His disciple and inviting me to follow Him and His disciples we all know. Maybe I'm not fit to be His disciple, after all. I've been so self-indulged with Sam and the Egans. Please! Who am I fooling? I mean, that's all you talk about, diary!

I'm so sorry, dear Lord. Shouldn't my main focus be You? Shouldn't You be my world? Not Sam, not the Egans, not this diary that's become my secret confidante. That should be You, Lord!

I've put You second to everything and everyone. You, who gave me my very life—my very existence, who died an excruciating and long death to pardon this sin I'm committing now. I'm so sorry, Lord Jesus. I don't know if I shall ever make rank as Your disciple, but may I ask You to, please, forgive me?

In John 13:34–35 (GNT), Jesus said, "And now I give you a new commandment: love one another. As I have loved you, so you must love one another. If you have love for one another, then everyone will know that you are My disciples."

I do love you, Lord, with all my heart. With Your love, I can love everyone.

Monday, December 24, 1877
Christmas Eve

Sam and the boys took the horses out for miles off the property to chop down a fir tree at Sarah's insistence on having a Christmas tree. Mr. Kane is selling candles for Christmas trees and counterweighted candle holders which are weird looking but work great. They are metal holders affixed atop a wire stem with a kink in it near the top to hook onto a tree branch. At the bottom of the stem is a weight, a red-painted ball of clay. It holds the candles perfectly firm on the tree!

We've but a few candles on our tree. Sarah and I twisted some colorful yarn together for garland. It's cute! I also taught them to pop corn (in the Dutch oven), which the boys are still munching on now. It's a hit! With needle and thread, we've strewn the popcorn with cranberries into long garlands as well, a family tradition from my clan.

Tuesday, December 25, 1877
Merry Christmas!
We spent Christmas day in the Egan home.

I love a white Christmas but am trying not to recall too much from Christmases with my family in my time. I'm really missing my real family right now.

Christmas with the Egans was simple and peaceful.

Sam and Sarah have tucked away the cheque until they can get to the bank to verify it is genuine and safe to deposit. So, still strapped for cash, gifts were scarce but very meaningful.

Sam made Sarah a beautiful wooden jewelry box. He carved her initials on the inside. He said it is for when they have money in the bank; he'll buy her some beautiful jewelry like she once had.

Gunnar gave Pa (I mean, Sam!) a sketch from a Montgomery Ward catalogue of a pistol (I forget what kind he said it was) that he wants to buy Pa when he gets his share of their money. I suppose that's honorable enough. Gunnar means well.

Sarah gave Gunnar a new Bible she wants him to start reading on his own. She expects his reading to improve as well as his character. I tried not to laugh.

And with the old grocery money she secretly saved, Sarah also bought Paul a gift. Can you guess? A new saddle!

I gave to Sam, Sarah, and the boys, two wool blankets that took me most of the year to complete. They love how heavy and warm they are. Sam and Sarah's blanket is white with red trim and the boys' is all red with white trim.

Then Sarah pulled out a bundled burlap sack tied with string from under the tree and handed it to me with a smile. I opened it to find a beautiful, heavy cloak. It was dark blue with black piping embroidered around the collar in the loveliest design. It had a deep hood too.

"I made this for you," Sarah said, "so you won't be cold doing the chores this winter. We never stopped praying that you would return to us."

I gave her a big hug.

We sat around the hearth and read Scripture, enjoying some fine, hot butter rum Sarah made special. What a treat! What really warmed my heart was what Sarah read: "We love Him, because He first loved us" (1 John 4:19, KJV).

I couldn't help but reminisce to the one Christmas I had in my former life that I will never forget.

It was the one I always described as the closest I will ever get to experience what the first Christmas must have felt like—the night Jesus was born. It was our first Christmas in the Philippines. My father had been transferred there in his job with the Navy; and so we went. I relayed as much of it as I comfortably could to the Egans.

"I lived once where people were very, very poor," I began with caution. "On Christmas Eve, my family was traveling (in a van but I omitted that) to collect my sister who was visiting (from the airport, but I didn't say that either).

"On the ride home, we saw people walking down the side of the road in complete silence. Each one carried a single glowing candle. No one spoke. No one sang carols. You could have heard a pin drop. It was so quiet. All these people, young and old, moved in procession like the three wise men in reverent silence.

"Then we passed their destination: the hillside of a church covered with people, all holding candles. They lit up the slope like a giant Christmas tree! The thing I remember most was passing an old woman sitting inside what (to me) looked like a big crate she may have lived in. This woman appeared to have nothing! Yet on a makeshift table in front of her stood tall her glowing candle. She somehow made sure she had it to honor our Lord," I ended.

Did I say she had nothing? She had everything. Everything that mattered; she had Jesus. These Pilipino people completely recognized the true meaning of Christmas. This one Christmas Eve was in every respect truly the "O' Holy Night, O' Night Divine." I know I will probably never again experience a Christmas like that: when I was twelve years old in the Philippines. But that's another story.

However, Christmas with the Egans was just a little bit close.

Tuesday, January 1, 1878

I can't believe it's 1878! The Egans are making plans to build onto the house now with their new fortune (from you know who). There will be a new room for Gunnar since I took his when I got here, which he'll never let me forget. Sam is also having a bunkhouse made so he can hire a dozen vaqueros. Until now, the three hired hands have been sleeping in the barn loft.

Then, tonight at supper, Sam and Sarah announced another construction to commence.

"A schoolhouse!" Sarah exclaimed, across the table from me. "So you can teach Paul and Gunnar and some of the neighbors' children perhaps. That is, if you'd like to. I've spoken to the Henkels and the Townsends. Both families wish their children to attend. Town is too far for them to walk and still have time to complete their chores after. They were never fond of Ms. Schumacher. Folks are beginning to complain about her ways."

I was stunned. Am I ready for this?

Sam just came in to put logs on my fire. He asked why I was still awake and how I liked the idea of being an *on-site* (my words) teacher. I told him that I still felt funny about living permanently with them. He knows why.

"You know," he said, "you've gotta stop feeling like you don't belong here and just decide that you do."

He patted my shoulder and walked out with a, "Go to sleep."

Oh, boy.

Thursday, February 7, 1878

I know it's been awhile but it's been very busy with trying to plan a curriculum for my new pupils once the schoolhouse is built.

We've had a new visitor of late: a white dog with a blondish tint to his short, floppy ears and coat; a fluffy, gleaming white tail that curls up; big paws; and the most unusual slanted, pale-blue eyes. He looks like he might be a husky-lab or retriever mix. He's such a beautiful dog! For a stray, I don't know how he keeps his white coat clean. None of the neighbors claim him. It's a mystery where he comes from. One of the new vaqueros, Alberto, suggested that he might have been let off the train by a traveler who could no longer care for him.

The mysterious dog started showing up on the ranch sporadically at first, but now he is around every day. At night, he looks like a ghost when he comes into view. When we were discussing names for him, I took the risk of telling the boys that he made me think of Casper the Friendly Ghost.

"There are no friendly ghosts," Gunnar retorted.

"Casper!" Paul shouted, beaming.

Paul has been tirelessly trying to pet Casper, but the timid dog won't allow anyone to come more than two feet from him, although he will gladly accept any food one lays out.

17

Reverend Bergie

Sunday, Feb 17, 1878

Reverend Bergdahl. Folks endear him with the name Reverend Bergie for the sweet man he is. The reverend is a quiet sort of man. Stout and jolly, he walks with a cane due to stray shrapnel that pierced a house-turned-hospital during the war while he was praying over a dying Yankee. He wears round spectacles that rest on rosy, bulbous cheeks. His eyes, like two blue buttons, smile at you with serenity. He speaks with a thick accent. Some say he is from Germany, others say he's from Sweden or Switzerland. But no one thinks it is fitting to ask him.

Thus, no one in Barlow knows anything about Reverend Bergie's background. He appears to have no family either. No wife, children, father, mother, sibling, nor any distant relation to speak of. He lives all by himself in a little house behind the church.

Well, I had to call on him about some other distress of late that I hadn't the morale to reveal to you, diary. Actually, it was Sarah who encouraged me to talk to R. Bergie. She said he could bring me peace and understanding. And that he did.

Whenever anyone has a problem they can't handle, they take it to the reverend. Often when church ends and the congregation departs, I can hear his cheery, baritone voice tell someone, "All-vighty, let us call in zee Lord and get to zee heart of zee matta."

Now it was my turn. In service today, the reverend ended his sermon from the book of Luke in which Jesus instructs us: When giving a lunch or dinner, not to invite the people we know, love or want to impress. Rather, invite the poor, the crippled, the lonely, and the helpless—ones who cannot pay us back. And we will be blessed (Luke 14:12–14 GNT).

After we sang "Amazing Grace" and "Bringing in the Sheaves" (sometimes I feel like I'm on *Little House on the Prairie*) and everyone had gone, I approached the reverend who was also preparing to leave.

I told him that I had some frightful dreams about where I came from. There were of all kinds of natural disasters in them: tsunamis (I had to explain what they were), earthquakes, and tornados that killed many people all over the world. I saw people die horrible deaths. It was such an upset.

He told me that, right off, it reminded him of the book of Revelations and he asked if I had read it. I had read some of it but not all. Well, he said it was about a time to come when most people no longer worship God or obey His commandments but instead worship other gods and idols. Since Adam and Eve, mankind has turned from God time and time again. And God has been trying to get us back because He loves us so.

But God gave us free will and is very patient. But there will come a time when He will have to call it a night and bring His children home—whoever wants to be with Him. I mean, who wouldn't want to?

Still I was troubled and asked R. Bergie, "How could a God who loves us so much send anyone to an eternal hell?"

"Vell, He is not. Gott vants to give life eternal to everyone. He vants everyone to come home to Him," was his answer. "But if somevone valks avay from Gott, from life itself, razher zhan to Him, vhere else can zhey go? It's really a choice ve make, Ms. Twining."

I've often wondered if, at some point in eternity, even hell might return to God. But that's going way off the radar! Oops! I wrote *radar*. Since I've been having these dreams, I've been remembering modern things. *Modern* as in my time. Since I've been here, I've gotten so used to considering things in 1877 modern. Wow! What a concept.

Anyway, R. Bergie asked me where I was from, which made me stutter, but all I revealed was California, nothing more.

Then he asked me something I thought very poignant: "To people from vence you come, is Gott central to zheir lives?"

"Well"—I dropped my head—"I suppose to some, but not everyone."

He told me not to worry myself. He said when things happen, such as natural disasters, we don't know if they are necessarily caused by God or not, but of one thing we can be certain: No matter what happens, God is with us. We can always depend on Him.

I can also vouch for You, Lord. As Psalm 63:7 (GNT) puts it, "Because You have always been my help."

That is sure the truth!

"Trust Gott," Reverend Bergie told me with the deepest endearment. "Because He sees vhat ve cannot."

He reminded me of Isaiah 55:8–9 (GNT). Here it is in my Bible:

> "My thoughts," says the LORD, "are not like yours, and My ways are different from yours. As high as the heavens are above the earth, so high are My ways and thoughts above yours."

Walking out of the little church, R. Bergie added that when folks lose everything they have, God will fill them back up with something new and wonderful, if they'll let Him.

I started away from the church and stopped to watch the old reverend turn toward his home. His gate was slow as he put cane first then feet. And I couldn't help but wonder: had he been one of those folks?

Wednesday, Feb. 20, 1878

I pondered my conversation with Reverend Bergie today when I accompanied Gunnar to catch some fish for supper. We walked along the river bank, looking for a good spot. Casper, who had been following at a distance, had now caught up. I thought how sad it is (and maybe makes God sad too) how much we take Him for granted. Just the fact that we're here! That we exist! I mean, He didn't have to create us. At all.

Every day that we wake up, why don't we thank the Lord for each new day? He didn't have to give it to us. Even if we lose everything we have, we still have our very being and we'll always have Him. Yet how much is He thanked? How often is He disregarded?

To treat God like that is like moving into someone's house (rent free), deciding never to leave, eating all their food, using all their things, but all the while completely ignoring that kind person! Don't ya think? I mean, how rude and ungrateful would that be?

God Himself is our greatest blessing!

If He were anything less than the perfect Creator He is, of perfect and eternal love and perfect justice (study creation itself), we would be or maybe we wouldn't be at all!

I know there are arguments that usually include the suffering people go through in this world which I'd hate to blame God for. Most people's suffering is caused by other people with ill intentions. And what about natural disasters? Death? Is death really a bad thing if it means spending eternity with God and our loved ones? Sadness in death is really of the living, not the deceased.

If anything, I think of my family members who have passed on as looking down from heaven, saying, "Oh, those poor things down there. Can't wait till they can join us up here and really live!"

When my mother died of cancer, strangely I never felt that she was really gone. She still filled my heart. I had feared that it would feel like a big emptiness in my spirit that I would never be able to bear, but it never did. It has been said there is a void in our hearts that only God can fill. But most people try to fill it with everything and everyone but God.

I guess there is only so much that we as human beings will ever be able to understand about God.

"We really have no idea." I heard myself blurt out as Gunnar hooked a line with a sacrificial worm that wiggled helplessly.

Then he threw the thing into the rushing creek with his eye across the bank, determined to catch sight of our now mutual bear friend.

"What!" he snapped. I had drifted off into deep thought again.

"I mean, like, think about it—" I started but he cut me off.

"You're talking strange again," he scoffed.

"Huh?"

"You're starting to say 'I mean' and 'like' inappropriately as when you first appeared," he furthermore assessed.

This struck me, like my writing *radar* in you the other day, diary. Remember?

"You sound stupid when you talk such," he added, insult to injury.

"Well, I'm sorry!" I exclaimed, exasperated. "Anyways—"

"A-ny-*way*!" he cut in again. "It's no wonder Ms. Schumacher fired you."

"Hey! 'I take no sass but 'sasparilla,'" I chided him and went on. "What I mean to say is this…"

Well, I tried to continue but had lost my train of thought, what with all this nonsense.

However, it returned to me that night when we all sat around the hearth, Sarah and I sewing. Ironically, I was mending one of Gunnar's shirts. I wanted to sew his sleeves together.

"We really have no idea how lucky we really are," I broke the silence.

"You said 'really' twice in one sentence!" Gunnar yelled from his room. "Don't allow her to teach us, Ma!"

Sewing the toes of his own stockings, Paul giggled uncontrollably. But I ignored them both and explained that I was referring to God and the realization I had after my talk with Reverend Bergie.

"I mean," I repeated just as Gunnar emerged. He hissed at me like a snake, but I continued. "We just have no idea how lucky we are that God is who He is."

"Oh, we know." Sam smiled.

"And we have known and believed the love that God hath to us," Sarah quoted 1 John 4:16.

"But, I mean, He could have been any way at all. What if He didn't love us? What if He was dishonest or conniving or anything less than the perfect God He is? Our very existence depends on this! I mean, what if our God was one that was evil? I mean, you know? When you really, really think about it, we cannot even begin to comprehend how lucky we really, truly are that He is who He is!"

"You said 'I mean' four times more and 'really' three." Gunnar counted. I threw his shirt at him since I was done with it anyway. He appraised my work.

"She stitched my sleeves adjoined!"

Ha!

Here it is, the Psalm 63:3–4 (GNT): "Your constant love is better than life itself, and so I will praise You. I will give You thanks as long as I live; I will raise my hands to You in prayer."

Thank you, Lord God, for everything. Even Gunnar. Brat.

18

Where God Wants Me

Monday, March 4, 1878

Casper is sitting outside my window tonight. He has just begun this habit. I wonder if it is because my light always burns the longest at night? It shines on him, I can see. He is curled up asleep on the ground.

It's useless to try to coax him inside. He just won't come in the house despite feeding him daily. What happened to this poor dog? What is his story, I wonder? Before I go to sleep at night, I tell him I love him and smack kisses to him from my window. Oh, Casper. Why are you so afraid? I read to him Psalm 31:14–15 (GNT): "But my trust is in You, O LORD; You are my GOD. I am always in Your care."

When I think about it, I can see myself in Casper. Here we care so much about him, and Paul loves him to pieces; yet Casper just can't seem to bring himself to trust us enough to tangibly accept our love, our hugs, and our home.

I think I'm the same way with the Lord. I want to believe that I trust God completely to take me where I truly belong, but I still can't stop feeling anxious about everything. It's as though I can't bring myself to allow God to completely touch my life. I keep taking it back, trying to figure things out for myself.

I see God reaching out to me as I back away from Him, saying "Renee, sweetheart, come here, my daughter. I love you! I won't hurt you. I want to help you and take care of your worries for you, sweetheart. Won't you let Me?"

What am I so darn afraid of? Why would I rather trust myself over trusting the all-knowing, the all-powerful? Am I stupid? Or crazy? I guess, both.

I even see Casper in Sam and Sarah, a little, as they second guess their decisions on how and when to spend their new money. That's why it's taken Sam this long to hire up to eight vaqueros and build a bunkhouse. Hmm, I wonder if God sent Casper to teach us how trusting we should be of Him? Well, Casper, you learn to trust us, and I'll learn to trust God. Deal?

He is sound asleep under my window now. Goodnight, sweetheart.

Friday, March 8, 1978

Spring is in the air! Flowers are budding on the trees. Sam and the boys have been playing baseball in the afternoons now that they have seven vaqueros to make up small teams. They put big rocks out for the base plates, and Sam made a wooden bat. And the balls? Sam also made them out of Colubrina snakewood that Smithy John had (the heaviest wood in the world, I'm told). Solid wood balls. Hit them and they might as well be cannon balls flying at ya. I whitewashed them and drew the red stitching (for which I had to make more red dye from the ol' cochineal bugs from the cactus).

Sam mentioned to me that even the British redcoats dyed their red coats with dye from the cochineal a century ago. Where cactus grows in England, I'll never know!

....

Friday, March 15, 1878

The bunkhouse is complete, and Sam has eight vaqueros working for him now. It is starting to look like a commune here. The schoolhouse is in preparation. I have put together a full year's curriculum, and we've already started having study sessions at either the Henkels or here. So far, so good.

For weeks now, Paul has been so frustrated with his efforts to pet Casper. He expected this progress to occur by now. But he burst into the house this afternoon, prancing about and shouting. He got Casper to take a bit of jerky right from his hand. At last. What joy!

"He still won't let me pet him, although," Paul frowned.

"Allow him more time," Sarah encouraged him.

Then Paul stuck his tongue out smugly at Gunnar who sat at the table with the funniest look of insult on his face in response. Up until now, Gunnar has been telling Paul to give it up and leave the dog to go on its way. You should have seen his face!

Saturday, March 16, 1878

A remarkable thing happened this morning while I was milking Clover. I felt a presence and looked behind me to see Casper sitting tall in the threshold of the barn. He just watched me. So I went back to milking when—you won't believe it. Casper walked up to a pale of warm milk set beside me and began to lap up some milk. He was so close, I could have put my arms around him, but I didn't dare move. Then he left.

Sunday, March 24, 1878

Well, the Egan boys and the vaqueros played baseball again today. I could not take my eyes off Sam running round the bases. This was the lightest and happiest I've ever seen him. It was as though a heavy load has been lifted from his shoulders—and from mine, as well. Maybe this is right. Maybe my home is here with the Egans. It may not make sense, but here I am. Perhaps in some strange way, it was as Chief Song Owl had said—Sam Egan has two wives.

But as I watched Sam run bases, I turned my mind to God in prayer:

"Dear Lord, I lift up this family to You. And I lift up myself to You, too. I ask that everything be done according to Your will and plan. You know what is right. Please take me, or keep me, where you want me to be. I let everything go to You, Lord. In Your holy name, Lord Jesus Christ, I pray. Amen."

Maybe this was where God wants me after all!

March 25, 1878

Renee got hit in the head with a ball yetserday and she wont waek up. Pa called on the doc. We are vary wurreed.

Paul

March 26, 1878

Renee is awak sumtims but not for vary long. Doc said she has sum thing call a concushin.

Paul

March 27, 1878

Renee died today in her sleep. We are vary sad.

Paul

19

I Am Where?

Thursday, November 7, 2013

I'm starting a new diary having lost my old one. This hurts. I can't write.

> Leave all your worries with Him, because He cares for you. (1 Pet. 5:7, GNT)

Friday, November 8, 2013

As you might guess, I am back in the 21st century. I want to write but it's really difficult. I'm so depressed, that I physically ache. In the mirror, I cannot recognize myself. My face looks weathered and wan. I look like I've lost ten pounds. I'm underweight. I guess from the drastic difference in my diet for so long. What no artificial anything and no preservatives will do to a person. Not to mention a lifestyle of physical labor. Come to think of it, I don't remember seeing anyone who was overweight the whole time I was there, in the 19th century. If anything, most people in Barlow looked like they could have used a few more pounds.

This is so hard to write. Oh, Lord, how can I go on?

> But His answer was: "My grace is all you need, for My power is strongest when you are weak." (2 Cor. 12:9–11 GNT)

Saturday, November 9, 2013

The last I remember is we were all laughing and having fun, playing baseball on the Egan ranch. I was on second base. Sam was the third baseman waiting to strike me out and Gunnar was at bat. As I leaned forward ready to run, Sam gave me a wink. And I thought, this must be true then, what God wanted—for me to be the second wife in Sam's family though in a strange, platonic sort of way.

Then Gunnar hit the ball and that was the last I remember.

I woke up in my bed back in my apartment. I think the day I returned here, Saturday, November 2, 2013, was the very next day after I had disappeared from here. Because I think it was a Friday night in the beginning of November when I originally disappeared, but I honestly can't remember. Strangely, when I awoke back here, my Bible was folded in my arms, and I wore the same clothes Sam had found me in. I'm so depressed. I can't do anything without crying.

It feels like I've been gone for a year. I feel I was really with the Egans for an entire year.

I loathe the use of electricity, especially electric lamps. In society it's unavoidable, but at home, at night, I use nothing but candles or oil lamps (unless reading presents too much of a challenge). There's nothing like the natural light of fire; no imitation will ever compare to God's own. No constructed light, no matter how advanced, will ever glow like the flame with its bright aura halo that glimmers with the color spectrum, its soothing shade of light, the unparalleled shadows it casts, and the tranquility it gives. It always transports me into another state of being, one that makes me feel closer to the Egans.

Speaking of fire, they fired me at work because of the "change in my behavior"; although, they acted like I had never left. Guess I cannot blame them, since I went in to work Monday after the weekend I had disappeared. Although, they were aghast at my appearance when they first saw me and thought I was sick.

I couldn't stop crying at the office. I couldn't focus and was making all kinds of mistakes. It was such a shock to be sitting in front of a computer again in a high-rise office of an entertainment law firm, redlining contracts, after what seemed like a year of milking a cow, collecting eggs, and tending a garden. I cannot tell you how jarring this was.

At first, I could hardly operate the computer. They thought I was playing around as I fumbled on the keyboard or tried to figure out how to work the new copier. I had gone so long without any technology whatsoever—no computer, no TV, no cell phone, nothing. And never once did I miss any of them.

Now that I think about it, I grew up without cell phones and computers and I'm so glad I did. I'm so glad. What, and miss out on life? When I think back on my childhood, my memories are of times spent with family and friends, of tinkering with toys or household things to create something new, playing with only the use of my imagination or playing board games with friends who actually have to sit with you at the same table to play them. (Wow, what a concept!) Or outside play sports or linking arms and swinging ourselves around in a game of crack the whip. We were always playing in someone's backyard or in the woods out back. Chasing lightning bugs at night in the summertime…I could go on.

It would make me sad if, at the end of my life, all I could recall looking back was spending most of my time staring at a phone screen. Or an iPad. It would be an unfortunate waste of life.

Life is precious, priceless. Days once spent are gone forever, never to be returned. God gave us a beautiful world to enjoy and explore. An old slogan comes to mind: "Life. Be in it."

You're a good listener, diary. Just like my old one. AH, I WANNA CRY!

Monday, December 16, 2013

I've been back a month now. I cannot stay away from Paramount Ranch; it's the closest I can get to being with the Egans. It hurts so much. Sitting on the railroad platform, I reflect on the dreams I had about Sam and Jethro when I was in 1877. Was everything that happened a dream? It must have been. What else could it have been?

Like a displaced ghost, I roam the aged wooden walkways lining the Western buildings of Paramount Ranch. It's like walking through a ghost town of Barlow. I look at the jail and envision Constable Dunn sitting on the porch cleaning his Colt 45. By an old shed, I can picture Smithy John making horseshoes for Sam. The general store makes me think of Mr. Kane laying eggs in the egg sale bucket.

That didn't sound right! LOL "L-O-L is not a word." This is the first I've laughed since I've been back.

Funny, don't you know, I remember years ago seeing an old Shirley Temple film (when she was real little) in which she tries to tell this crotchety lady (who reminds me of Ms. Schumacher) about an "amazing, egg-laying goose."

The lady retorts, "What's so amazing about an egg-laying goose?"

Little Shirley Temple looks up wide-eyed and asks in all earnestness, "Can you lay an egg?"

So cute.

Wednesday, January 22, 2014

Today is my mom's birthday. Happy Birthday, Mom!

Though most of my time of late has been preoccupied with feverish job hunting, I've found time to locate a few other historic sites to haunt that remind me of my life back in 1877.

In Agoura, there's an old adobe called the Reyes Adobe. When I walked into the guest bedroom of it, it was like walking into my old room at the Egans. I think it was the low ceiling and wood floors that especially made it seem so. And the position of the rope bed to the window.

There's also the Leonis Adobe Museum in Calabasas, still a ranch with live animals (though for representation's sake now) that, too, makes me feel back at home with the Egans again. They have so many things to see from those times. The same kind of wash ringer and board Sarah and I used, several wagons and carriages (even an old supply wagon like Sam's), and live ranch animals: longhorn steer, chickens, goats, horses, and the sheep Sam wanted but never got, save "Feliz". Oh, Feliz! I miss my baby girl! Perhaps I should inquire about a job here?

There's also the Stagecoach Inn Museum in Newbury Park that has an old schoolhouse just like the one in Barlow and a wooden pioneer house that resembles the Egans' home before they started adding onto it.

Between these two historic sites is the Chumash Indian Museum in Thousand Oaks that reminds me of Chief Song Owl and his tribe. You can tell this indeed was actual sacred land on which the Chumash lived thousands of years ago; you just feel it amid many oak trees that surround their life-like Chumash village. A dry riverbed that lines it makes me think of my bear friend by the creek.

Saturday, February 8, 2014

A weird and wonderful thing happened today. I was sitting by the creek at Paramount Ranch and I fell asleep. I had the most amazing dream about Jesus.

I was on the ground with this big, heavy cross on my shoulder. It was the garner of all my sins I ever committed and will yet commit. It was so heavy and bruising, I could not lift it. But I had to. Then Jesus came up to me ever so gently. There was so much pain in His eyes for me. He was feeling pain for me! There was not a hint of rebuke, judgment, or condemnation in His eyes. Just total empathy. He said something like, "Please, may I help you? Let me take this for you." And then He took the cross off of my shoulder and put it on His. He was not going to help me carry my cross; He was going to carry it for me, and suffer the torture and death that I was supposed to endure. Then I woke up. Or so I thought.

I woke up beside the creek and saw Jesus sitting right next to me. He said He'd been sitting there all along, even though I hadn't been able to see Him. He's been walking around with me every day, holding me by the hand even, but I had forgotten all about Him. I had stopped reading His Word. I was losing touch with Him.

He told me not to forget that He is always with me, even though I cannot see Him. That I don't have to ignore Him and go it alone. It pains Him to watch me stumble, trying to do things on my own. He wants to help me. To go through it with me. He wants me to share the experience with Him and allow Him to guide me through the life He made for me, all the way to His ultimate, eternal destiny He has in store. That was how He explained it to me.

He has been with me all this time, (within me, beside me, around me) just waiting for me to simply remember that He is there! I feel so stupid!

I reached out and hugged Him. I hugged Jesus! It was so real! I woke up (for real the second time) crying tears of joy!

Lord, forgive me! I never meant to forget You ever again. And I did. I forgot you. I pushed You into the background. I promise, I will never do that again. I will walk with You. I will talk with You about everything. From now on. I promise.

Here's the scripture! I'm looking right at it. It's staring me in the face.

> "I ask God from the wealth of His glory to give you power through His Spirit to be strong in your inner

selves, and I pray that Christ will make His home in your hearts through faith. I pray that you may have your roots and foundation in love, so that you, together with all God's people, may have the power to understand how broad and long, how high and deep, is Christ's love. Yes, may you come to know His love—although it can never be fully known—and so be completely filled with the very nature of God." (Eph. 3:16–19, GNT)

Saturday, March 1, 2014

I know it's been awhile but I've actually been quite busy. Not only am I talking the Lord's ears off so much that I think He may be avoiding me now, (just kidding, Lord), but I am working! I got a job! I'm the new administrative assistant at the Leonis Adobe Museum! I've also been teaching in the Children's Ministry at Gateway Church and Mercy Chapel in Agoura Hills. Both churches are very dedicated to helping others build true relationships with God. Everyone new in my life is like extended family to me now, just like back in good ol' Barlow. I'm making the dearest of new friends.

In our Ladies Hands On group, we've been busy with a lot of community activities, too, such as walking for the Relay For Life cure for cancer and cleaning up lawns and backyards for people less able. We make no-sew blankets and puts together bags of toiletries and treats for orphans, abused women, and hospice patients. Soon we'll be preparing a lot of stuffed stockings to send to the troops overseas for Christmas and putting gift boxes together for Operation Christmas Child.

And, through my work at the Adobe, I've found new people to crochet blankets for—children who benefit from the My Stuff Bags Foundation. I've also been able to help out with fundraisers for the Jennifer Diamond Cancer Foundation.

Though I've lived here for years, this is the first I have begun to get to know my township in the way I got to know the folks in Barlow. I'm getting to know neighbors and employees at the market, the bank, and the cleaners by name. Why had I never attempted to know them before?

Like in 1870s Barlow, the Lord has opened me up to folks here like I've not done since I was growing up in Hamilton, Maryland. Prior to Barlow, I was too caught up in my own life and routine to get to know anyone. And it was very lonely. Now, I am blessed with the joy of greeting a familiar face everywhere I go. Gee, what a concept!

Thursday, April 31, 2014

Though I feel I've done well in creating a new life for myself since I've been back, I still sometimes fall into bouts of depression. Deep down, I still feel my place is with the Egans. I wish I could go back. Every night since my return, I have tried to will myself back to them, hoping and praying that I would wake up to look into Sam's face again.

Why am I back here, Lord? Why did You send me there in the first place, if it was not meant to be? I just don't understand, Lord! Please help me to understand. I feel so empty again. I don't care if it might have been just a dream. I never wanted to wake up from it. You could have allowed that, Lord. You can do anything. See?

"To Him who by means of His power working in us is able to do so much more than we can ever ask for, or even think of:" (Eph. 3:20 GNT)

And yet: "Humble yourselves, then, under God's mighty hand, so that He will lift you up in His own good time." (1 Peter 5:6 GNT)

Okay, Lord. I will humble myself under Your mighty hand and trust You, Jesus. But I shan't write anymore in this diary. It just hurts too much.

Friday, December 4, 2015

Wow. It's been a long time, my friend. Well, never mind that. You won't believe what just happened today! See, last Sunday at church, Pastor B. said that when we're at our lowest point, that's when God cracks His knuckles and says, "I'm just getting started to do My best work." And how!

I was cleaning my apartment when the doorbell rang. There was a striking man, about my age, standing there looking apologetic with a small, wood-crafted box (a little bigger than a cigar box) with a lock on it.

He said, "I'm looking for a Ms. Renee Twining."

You're looking at her! I couldn't quite take my eyes off of him, really. He reminded me a little of Sam and, oddly, a bit like Paul too. But he was his own creature, all the same.

It seemed safe enough, so I let him in. He explained he came here to hand-deliver this box because it was irreplaceable.

I asked him what it was and he replied, "Well, that's the real mystery I was hoping you could help my family solve."

We sat down at a dark wood table I bought a while back that reminds me of the Egan's table and gives me the sense of eating with them still. I sometimes cry when I sit there. But not today.

He said, "Ms. Twining, my great-great-grandfather was a man named Paul Egan."

I almost fell off my chair.

"Oh, forgive me, my name is Sam Egan, Samuel Gunnar Egan. I was named after my great-great-great-grandfather, Sam, and my great-great uncle, Gunnar Egan."

I could tell he noticed I was in shock by the way he looked at me. I could not believe what I was hearing!

He went on to tell me he flew out here to personally bring me this box. It's been in his family for generations and has never been opened. It was forbidden in the will of great-great-great grandfather Sam who was one of the wealthiest ranch owners outside Barlow, Arizona. In fact, there's a town named Eganville where his ranch used to be.

When I heard this, I burst out laughing thinking about how much Sam had struggled while I was there. Eganville. The man looked at me funny. I apologized.

He went on to say that what his family did not understand was that the will forbade anyone to open this box and instructed that it be saved until December 4th, 2015 when it must be personally delivered to a Renee Twining of Agoura Hills, California. Everyone thought this Sam was crazy to search for me, but he committed to the task and tracked me down. He said he has been waiting for this moment his whole life.

This was Sam Egan's dying wish and his great-great-great-grandson of same name just had to oblige him. As he spoke, I examined the locked box he handed me.

"It's got a good lock," I noticed. "Looks like Smithy John made it."

This Sam dropped his jaw.

"That's right! How did you know that?"

"Huh?" I uttered, still enamored by the box.

"My dad told me that my grandfather told him that his granddad Paul said this lock was made by the blacksmith in town everyone called Smithy John."

I didn't know what to say next. But Sam excused me of the obligation by continuing.

"The box itself was made by Sam Egan."

Tears began to well up in my eyes. Dang glands!

"Ms. Twining, something my whole family's been dying to know. How are you connected to the Egans? Do you know why this box would be willed to you?"

I was without words and voice. What should I tell him? The truth? And what was the truth? Even I didn't know myself now.

"I-I'm not sure," I stuttered, "Why don't we try to open it and see what's inside?"

Before my eyes, Sam presented an old brass key.

"This was the one thing we were allowed to see but was always kept in a safe," he explained about the key.

He handed it to me, and I put it into the lock which clicked open with ease. The lid squeaked open with age. A musty smell filled my nostrils. I was flabbergasted by what lay inside.

"My diary!" I exclaimed before I could catch myself. Boy, it looked old.

I glanced at this Sam. As expected, he was giving me another strange look. He really was quite handsome.

"I mean, it looks like a diary I owned once," I restated.

"Okay, so whose diary was this?"

Sam picked it up and started thumbing through it! Dang, I wished I had gotten a lock back then! I nearly grabbed it from him, hoping his eyes wouldn't lay sight on my mentions of Chewbacca or Indiana Jones! How would I explain that?

"Oh, sorry. Forgive me. Do you mind?" he asked politely.

"Uhhhh…" I muttered.

Sam flipped back to the front.

"Well, it doesn't say who it belongs to."

Then his face froze on a page near the beginning. I froze too as he began to read it aloud.

"'My name is Sam Egan. This is my wife, Sarah. And what be your name, miss?'" He paused. "'Renee.' They looked at me.

It's obviously not a common name around here. 'Twining,' I added, as if that would make a difference."

He looked at me, stupefied. I just shrugged.

"Your," he uttered, "your great-great-great-grandmother?"

I just nodded. Why not?

"Wow!" he laughed, "So that's it!

They met your great-great-great-grandmother who you were named after, right? I mean, unless Twining is your married name. Is Twining your maiden name?"

"No. Yes!" I stammered. "Are you?"

"Am I…" Sam repeated.

"Married?" I could barely get out.

"Married? No, I'm, well, I'm divorced," Sam clarified, "My wife and I separated three years ago. It was mutual and I now have custody of our two children. Our son, another Paul, and our daughter, Sarah, named after—"

"Sam Egan's wife," I finished for him.

"Yeah. That's right."

I noticed his eyes were hazel like Sam's.

"Are you from Barlow? I mean, Eganville?" I asked him, trying not to giggle again.

"I'm from Pennsylvania," he answered, "from a small town nobody's ever heard of called Hobbs Forge."

That's where Sam's family—the Egan farm—was during the war! I wondered if this Sam even lived in their old, farm house? If it still stood? But I was too overwhelmed to ask.

"Oh," was all I could say, feeling a bit lightheaded.

There was a long silence.

"So, what kind of work do you do?" he broke it with.

"Well, I'm an admin at the Leonis Adobe Museum and I teach at my church's children's ministry. I'm thinking about pursuing a career as a history teacher perhaps."

"Oh, yeah? Hobbs Forge Christian School is hiring now. In fact, I'm the pastor of the church there."

"Is that I fact?" I gasped.

"Yeah." He smiled. "Coincidence, huh? God works in mysterious ways, doesn't He?"

I found myself getting lost in his face, then thought I felt a nudge from the Lord.

"Yes, He does." I heard myself concur.

Something slipped out of my diary onto the table: a thick, cardboard photograph of the Egans! They wore finer clothes. I'd never before seen Sam in a suit! He looked rather stiff in it, sitting in a chair. Ha, ha. Both Sam and Sarah looked the same, but the boys looked a little older and taller. None of them smiled though. They all looked so stern. And would you know? Paul sat on the floor, in front of them all, with his arm hugging Casper who looked as happy as could be.

Then it dawned on me: Chief Song Owl! Telling Sam that he had two wives. He was so adamant about it, but when I ended up back here, I figured he had been wrong. But what if Chief was right? What if he meant two wives of two Sam Egans in the same bloodline? If that's the case, could this have been God's plan all along? Could this be why He placed me back in time with the Egans whence I got hit in the head with Sam's deadly baseball only to return back here to meet Sam's descendant? Who's no longer married?

Guess I'll just have to be patient—and trust Him.

> I alone know the plans I have for you, plans to bring you prosperity and not disaster, plans to bring about the future you hope for. (Jer. 29:11, GNT)

I praise you, God, forever!

About the Author

Michele Fischer was born in Baltimore, Maryland but was destined to become a navy brat who spent four of her years growing up in the Philippines and one in England. She's been writing stories and acting since a child. To date, she has had articles published and originated several other manuscripts and screenplays. She studied creative writing in college and holds a BA in English and an AA in liberal arts.

Michele is also a professional actor and filmmaker who lives on the outskirts of Los Angeles County, California. Her pet sheep, Feliz, died during the production of this book. Michele plans to write a children's book about, and dedicated to, this very sweet and beloved animal.

More info:
michelefischer.net
9doorsfilms.com
Facebook: thebrandedheart
Twitter: 9doorsprods